D1130905
FOR GIRLS
1997
STORIES
PUZZLES
PIN-UPS
£4.75

inside

P 13

P 46

P 89

P 113

P 124

P 54

penny's place

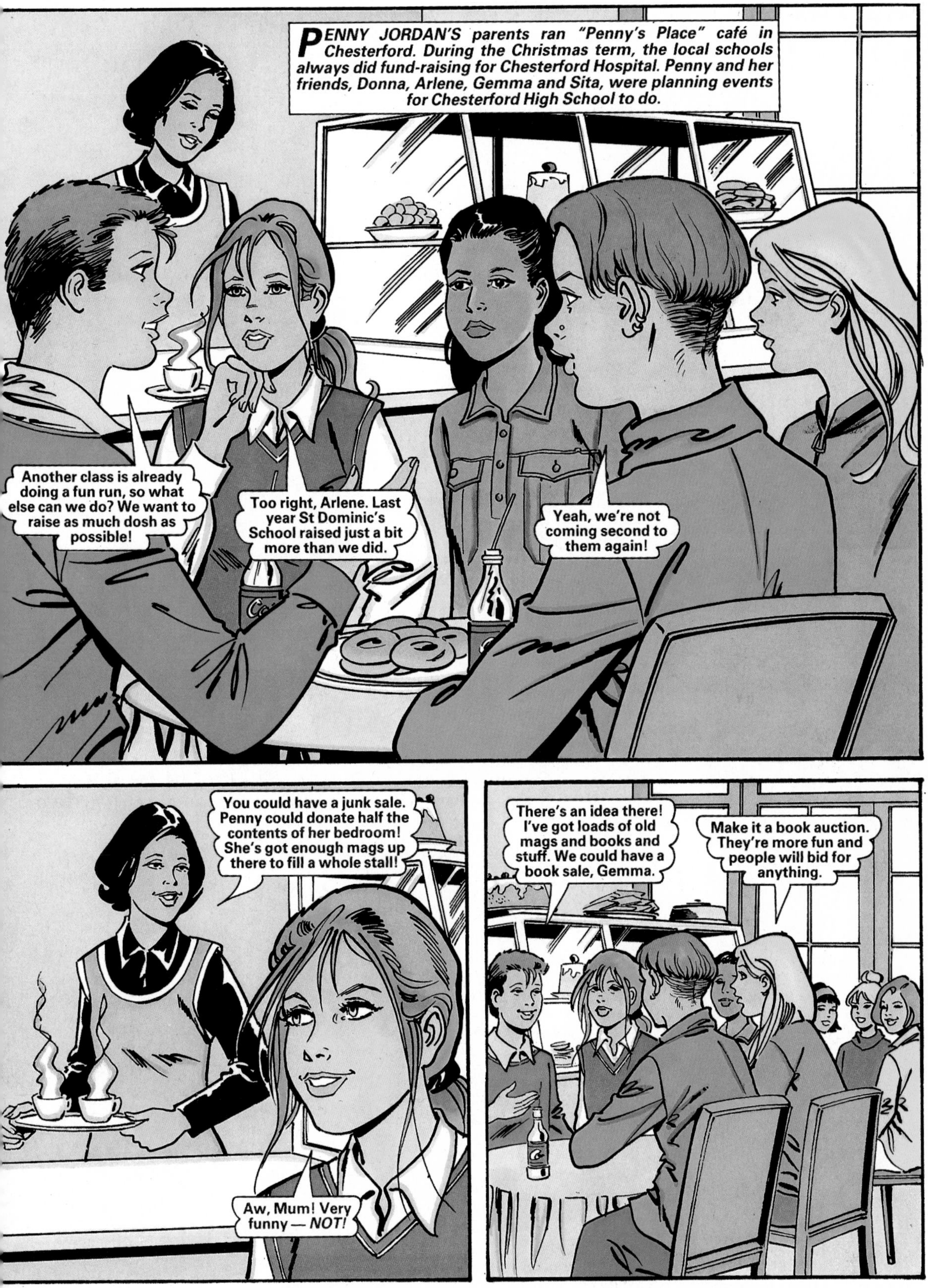

PENNY JORDAN'S parents ran "Penny's Place" café in Chesterford. During the Christmas term, the local schools always did fund-raising for Chesterford Hospital. Penny and her friends, Donna, Arlene, Gemma and Sita, were planning events for Chesterford High School to do.

Another class is already doing a fun run, so what else can we do? We want to raise as much dosh as possible!

Too right, Arlene. Last year St Dominic's School raised just a bit more than we did.

Yeah, we're not coming second to them again!

You could have a junk sale. Penny could donate half the contents of her bedroom! She's got enough mags up there to fill a whole stall!
Aw, Mum! Very funny — *NOT!*

There's an idea there! I've got loads of old mags and books and stuff. We could have a book sale, Gemma.
Make it a book auction. They're more fun and people will bid for anything.

Book auction? Bet that Chesterford High lot are trying to think up ways to beat us in the fund raising.
Pathetic, Harriet! A book auction won't do it. Selling a few tatty old books and comics — *BIG DEAL!*
WE'RE going to win again!

I didn't know there were any Dominics' Dimbos in here listening, Penny!
I wonder what ideas that lot have got that are so brilliant then?

Next day —
What's going on here? The school's roped off!
Here comes Dragon Draxler . . .

Attention, everyone! Due to a burst pipe in one of the upstairs rooms, there's considerable flood damage to two floors in the east wing.
Our form room's there! Maybe we'll get a holiday while they patch things up!

The wing will have to be closed for repairs for some time. Forms Seven A and Seven C will be going to St Angela's — and the rest of you to St Dominic's.
That's *US!* They're sending us to school with the Dominics' Dimbos. Gross!

So —
Oh, no! Not the High School Horrors coming here!
Hey, listen! We don't like it any more than you lot do! We don't *WANT* to be here!
Conditions will be cramped, so we must all put in a lot of effort to make this work. Now, I'd like you to make our guests from the High School feel welcome!
Fat chance!
And we hope you High School pupils will join in the carol singing that we're doing to raise funds for the hospital!
Well, well! So now we know what their plans are!
Carol singing won't beat Chesterford's fun run! And we've got the book auction, too!
Well, we've got a raffle going — and the tickets are already selling fast, so get ready for your school to lose again!
The timetable says we've got biology next. Where's their bio lab?
We'll have to ask.

The bio lab? Over there.
Best get a move on. Old Williams doesn't like pupils being late!

Soon —
And what, may I ask, are *YOU* doing here?
This is the art block! Those girls sent us to the wrong place! The rats!

Later —
Take your seats! I will *NOT* tolerate lateness!
They're laughing at us, rotten lot! They did this on purpose!

After school —
What a day!
Hey, what are those St Angela's lot doing hanging about here?
Hoi! Dominic Dimbos! Off to practise your carol singing, then?

D'you mind! We're from the High School!
Even worse! St Angela's are going to raise the most money this year so you lot can give up now!
Nice girl — *NOT!*

That weekend —
When you see the St Angela's lot, Dominics' girls don't look so bad. We've got to make our book auction the greatest! Here come some people now.

And what am I bid for this schoolgirl annual from nineteen forty seven? Do I hear fifty pence? Thank you, Madam! Any advance on fifty pence? One pound! Now, who'll give me two pounds?
Sold to the lady in blue for two pounds! Now — ten comics. Who'll start the bidding at twenty pence?
Arlene's brilliant! A natural!
fter the ction —
We've made forty six pounds seventy five! That's excellent! What a brilliant start to our fund raising!
Back at St Dominic's —
We drew our raffle at the weekend. It took over sixty pounds — so you're not winning. Sorry, Penny!
Well, we've our fun run to come, Harriet!
And we've our carol singing!
hen, later —
That Chesterford girl, Arlene Fletcher, is playing well. We've a match against St Angela's this Saturday and one of our team's off sick. I'll ask her to play!
You'll play for ST DOMINIC'S?
Aw, it's just a game of hockey, Donna — and I love hockey! Anyway, I can't stand the St Angela's lot! I'll enjoy the chance to beat them!

Then, on Saturday —
You're the drip who did the book auction, aren't you? My mum tricked you! That annual she bought was worth forty quid — and you let it go for two! Ho! Ho!
That's not fair! It's the hospital that's the loser!

Later, on the pitch —
OW!
That St Angela's sneak has whacked Harriet on purpose, when she knew the ref wasn't looking.

Right! We'll sort them out!
Nice one, Arlene!
Go for it, Arlene!
GOAL!

Three-one to us — and you scored two of them!
You were brilliant, Arlene!
Seems you're getting on okay with the Dominics now, Arlene!
They're not so bad when you get to know 'em, Penny. Wait for me — I'll get changed and be right with you.

he changing room —
What are those two St Angela's girls saying?
I've found out the exact route the Dominic Dimbos are going to use for their carol singing.

Nice one! All we have to do is go round the same route — but an hour earlier!
Sneaks! I'm not going to let them get away with this! I'll warn Harriet. They can go round *TWO* hours earlier.

Good tidings we bring, to you and your kin . . .
This is the last street — And we've done really well!

The St Angela's lot haven't done well! *LOOK!*

I've had a bunch of you schoolkids collecting for the hospital, not an hour ago! I'm not giving *TWICE!*
Ha! Ha! Ha!

Hope that your carol-singing wasn't going to be your main fund raiser, Angies. Cos, if it was, you've lost *BIG* time!
HUH!

Thanks, you lot!
You helped us — so now we'll all join you on your fun run!
Excellent! The more bods the better!

So, next day —
Our new pals drummed up a whole lot of support. This is going brilliantly!

And, after the run —
It doesn't matter which school raised most money.
Yes who cares? It's all for the hospital! Mum, bring on the doughnuts. This is a celebration!

Merry Christmas to all of us!
Friends at last!
Yeah, kind of a shame we have to go back to our own school on Monday.

Hey, that's right! Don't forget we're playing you Chesterford lot at netball on Tuesday. Prepare to get clobbered!

What? *NO WAY!*

In your dreams!

Here we go! Rivals again! Ha! Ha! Ha!

THE EN

LUCK OF THE DRAW
27
4
16
ONE day at Mel's —
Dad and I have been talking, Mel. We've decided you've done so well in your exams at school, you can have a lottery ticket.
Yeah, Mum? Brilliant!
This is great. Imagine if I won. Even enough to buy a new stereo would be mega.
Right, what numbers shall I have? My birthday, the house number, the phone number? Oh, I just don't know.

So —
Help, Lisa. I've no idea what numbers to pick!
Well, why don't you pick a day and see what numbers jump out at you?
Hmm! Yeah, I'll do that. Saturday'll be a good day.
So —
Hey! Look at that number plate, MEL SEVEN. Seven. That'll do for my first number.
49
And it's parked outside house number forty-nine. That can be my next number.
And —
Can I see how much we bought, Mum.
Sure, love!
Mum bought fourteen things. That's another number.

Then —
Oops!
Careful, Melanie.

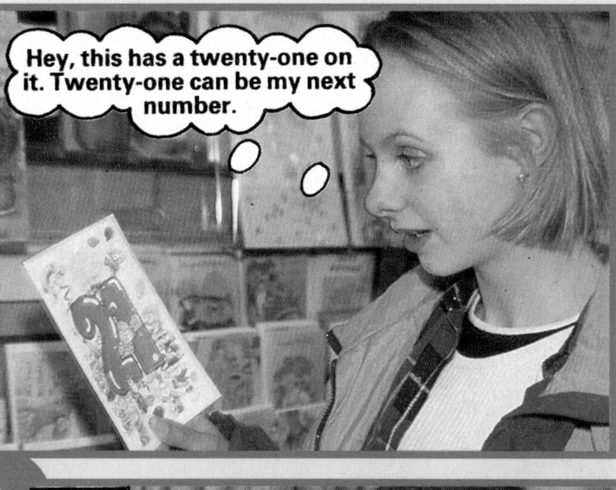
Hey, this has a twenty-one on it. Twenty-one can be my next number.

I'll have to ring Lisa and tell her how ace her idea is. I've got four numbers just going to the shops.

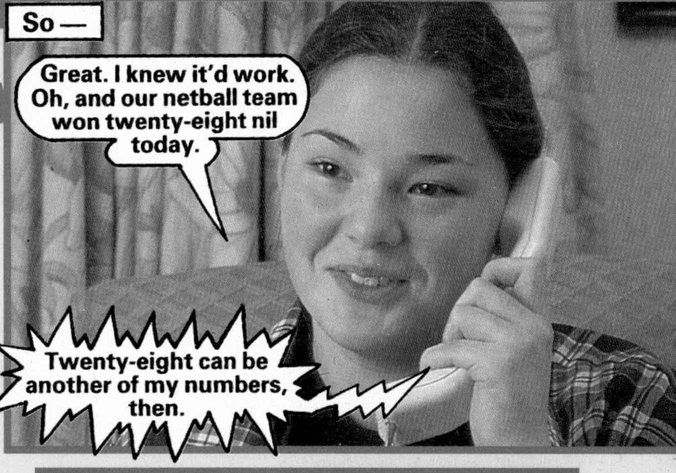
So —
Great. I knew it'd work. Oh, and our netball team won twenty-eight nil today.
Twenty-eight can be another of my numbers, then.

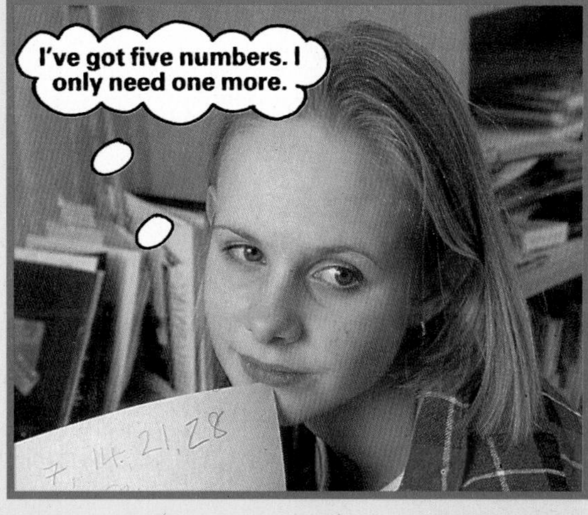
I've got five numbers. I only need one more.

I know! Our house number, thirty-five. All the numbers are a multiple of seven. That *HAS* to be lucky!

Here we are, Dad. I've done my numbers for the lottery.
Put them on the unit, love. I'll have to finish this job first.

So —
Phew. I'm glad that's finished.
Don't forget the lottery tickets, Mike.
Especially mine, Dad.

Later —
It's almost time for the lottery draw. Dad's still not back. I wonder what's happened?

But —
What a let down. I didn't even get one number.
Neither did your dad and I. Where could he have got to?

At last —
Sorry, love, the car broke down and I was too late to get the tickets. But I did get you a scratch card instead.
Thanks, Dad.

I don't believe it! I've won!
You have? How much?

One pound. That's enough to try again next week!
THE END.

Gemma

SALLY FOSTER'S mother was taken ill —

Is Mum going to be all right, Dad?

She'll be in good hands at the hospital, Sally and Gran's coming to stay, so she'll help us.

We'll have to keep Gemma in my room out of the way as usual then, won't we? It's a shame Gran's allergic to dogs.

That's all right when Gran comes for the day, but she's staying this time. We'll have to make arrangements for Gemma.

Make arrangements? What do you mean, Dad?

Leave it to me, Sally and don't worry.

A few minutes later —

The Johnsons over in Calford have agreed to look after Gemma while Mum's in hospital.

No, Dad, no! I can't bear it if she goes away.

It's hard for me, too, love, but there's nothing we can do. Mum wants Gran to be here.
So, later that day —
Bye, Gemma. See you soon.
I love her so much.
Gran came to stay, but Sally missed Gemma. The following week —
I miss Gemma. I miss her every minute.
Meanwhile, at the Johnsons' house —
I wish she would eat something. I think she's missing Sally.
GEMMA
And, a few days later —
She's got so much thinner. Do you think we should phone the Fosters?
No, I don't think we should bother them. They have enough problems, don't they? They've to visit the hospital every day.

t, a week later —
Gemma's run away. We've looked everywhere but there's no sign of her. Oh, we *ARE* sorry, Sally.
We'll find her. We must. She'll be trying to get home, won't she?
Calford's fifteen miles away, though.
So —
That's the advert placed in our paper then, as well as the Calford one.
We'll get these posters and ads in as many shop windows as possible. I'll take one to the vet's as well.
o, soon —
course, Sally, we'll do what we n to help. Put a poster on the ting room wall there and we'll ll our clients to look out for her.
Thanks, Mr Wilson.
HAVE YOU SEEN THIS DOG?
Over the next few days —
I dreamed of finding Gemma straight away, but nobody seems to have seen her. Maybe she didn't come this way after all.
At the weekend —
Good news, love. Mum's coming out of hospital tomorrow. She'll be back to her old self in a week or so.
That's great, Dad.
So Gran will go home and I could have Gemma back. But I can't, can I, because she's gone.

Meanwhile, many miles away —
Get off the road, you stupid dog!
And —
Look! There's a dirty old dog by our dustbin. Go on, get away!
Gemma was so hungry and had nowhere comfortable to rest —
Weeks passed, but Sally never gave up hope —
We're still doing what we can, Sally. I have all the local farmers keeping an eye open for me. They'll phone me if they spot her.
Thank you, Mr Wilson.

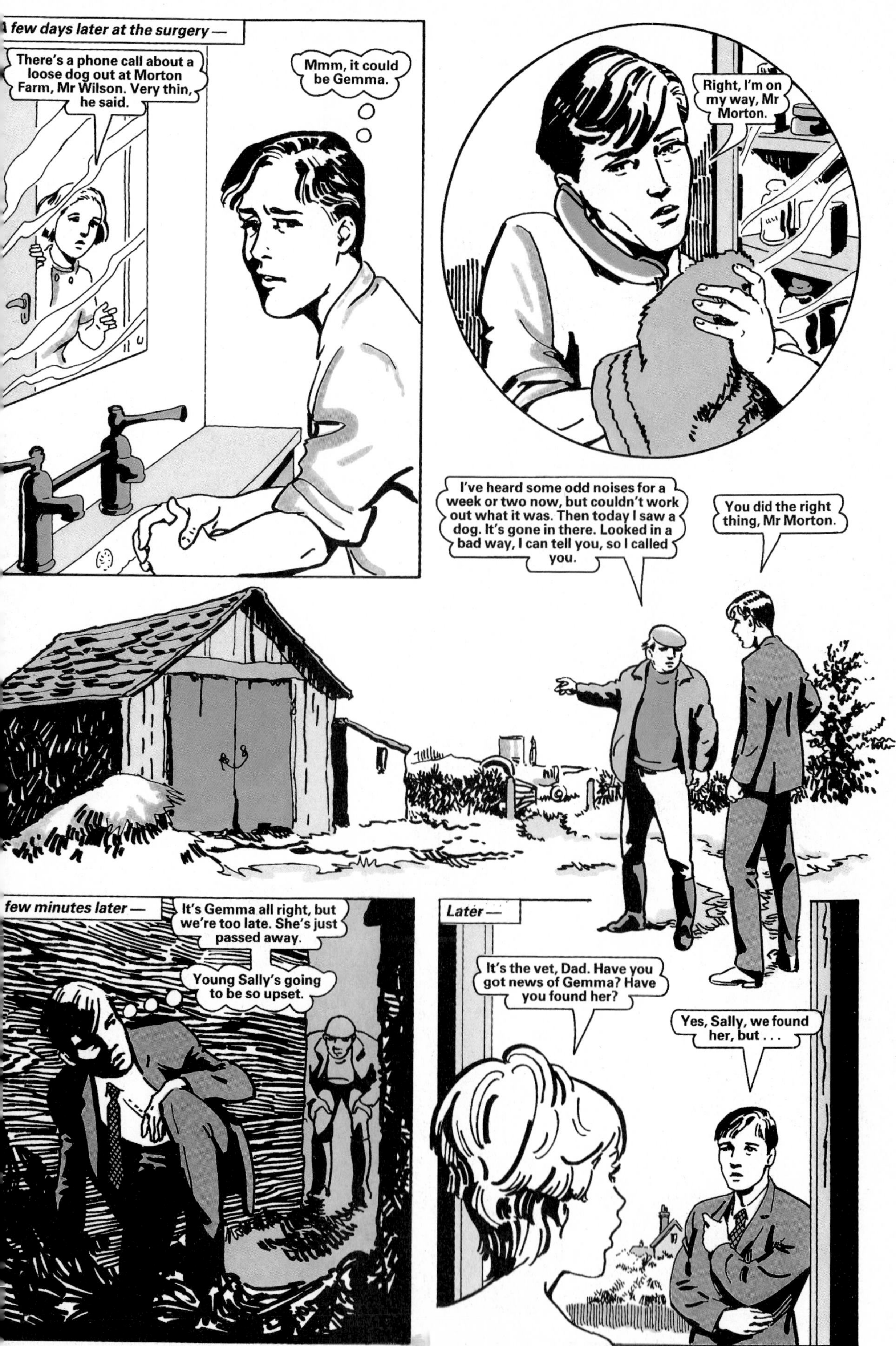
A few days later at the surgery —
There's a phone call about a loose dog out at Morton Farm, Mr Wilson. Very thin, he said.
Mmm, it could be Gemma.
Right, I'm on my way, Mr Morton.
I've heard some odd noises for a week or two now, but couldn't work out what it was. Then today I saw a dog. It's gone in there. Looked in a bad way, I can tell you, so I called you.
You did the right thing, Mr Morton.
few minutes later —
It's Gemma all right, but we're too late. She's just passed away.
Young Sally's going to be so upset.
Later —
It's the vet, Dad. Have you got news of Gemma? Have you found her?
Yes, Sally, we found her, but . . .

I can tell from your face. I know what you're going to say.
I'm sorry, Sally, Gemma didn't make it.
She found a place on a farm to have her puppies, but she wasn't strong enough to feed them. This one survived, though. Here you are, Sally.
A puppy? Gemma's puppy?
Oh, Gemma, I'll always miss you. I'll never, ever forget you, but I'll love your puppy for you.
THE EN

STAGE SCHOOL

THERE was a new girl, Jocasta, at the Madame Celeste School where Nicky Carr and Suzie Mantle were pupils.
Very good, Jocasta!
The new girl IS good, isn't she, Nicky?
Maybe not quite as good as she thinks she is, Suzie!
I'VE won several ateur talent shows. I KNEW I'd be taken on here!
I see what you mean, Nicky. She's a bit full of herself.
A BIT? If she's not careful, she'll turn out as big a show-off as grotty Gavin Mellor! Pity I have to star in the same TV soap as him!
Later —
Who are those men with Madame Celeste?
Dunno — but she doesn't look happy.

Bad news, girls. Those surveyors tell me our theatre is unsound. Until the work's done we can't use the building! I do not have enough funds available at the moment.
I know there are a few cracks in the walls, but I didn't think it was serious, Madame!
In the common room —
We can't do without our theatre!
I've an idea! We could put on a show to raise funds for the building work!
We'd have to hire a theatre to do it.
I don't mind taking part. People will pay more to see a *REAL* star, like me.
We'll have to make it a *BIG* theatre, then, to fit your fat head in, Gavin Mellor!
Get lost, Nicky!
Soon —
A show wouldn't raise enough money, girls, but it would be a start.
We thought we'd put on an open air show first, Madame, to advertise the event.
The market square is always crowd on Saturday — and the more peop that know about the show, the bett Please say 'yes', Madame!
Madame thought it over and agreed.
We've got a good crowd!
Everyone's here to see *ME*!

Ooh! It's Leanne from 'Market Place'!
Can I have your autograph?
That's put Gavin in his place. Nicky's much more popular than him!
The show began.
Jocasta loves an audience!
Wow! Suzie, look at that girl over there, dancing to the music! She's *BRILLIANT!*
Excuse me! We've been watching you dance. What's your name?
Oh! Er — L-Lucie. You're on the telly, aren't you?
I'm Nicky Carr and this is Suzie Mantle. Lucie, we think you're a great dancer. Where did you learn?
Nowhere! I just like dancing! I dance to tapes and stuff at home. I do my own thing!

You've got real talent, Lucie. You should be at our Stage School!
Suzie's right. It's for talented kids like you. Why don't you audition?
I CAN'T!
The school's on West Street. Come on Monday morning. HEY! WAIT! LUCIE!
Why did she run off like that? She looked really upset!
Hey, Nicky! Tickets for the show are selling well.
Excellent. That's what we wanted
Later, back at stage school —
I hope Lucie will come. Haven't you got to do a personal appearance on Monday, though, Nicky?
Not till the afternoon. Grotty Gavin and I are booked to open a new supermarket.
Gosh, the exciting life you top stars lead!
You're jealous, cos YOU'D like to spend a whole afternoon with Gavin — NOT!
On Monday —
It's past twelve and there's no sign of Lucie. She can't be interested in coming here.
But why? It would be the perfect chance to develop her talents. Madame's a wonderful teacher! If only we could talk to her again!

We don't even know her full name, let alone where she lives.
I'm not having Creepy Carr hogging all the attention this afternoon. I'll fix *HER!*

Outside —
Good! Our limo's a couple of minutes early. Nicky isn't out yet. This is my chance!
Nicky Carr sends her apologies, but she's not feeling well. She won't be coming. It's only me.

HEY! The limo's gone without me! This'll be that skunk Gavin's doing!

I'll ring for a taxi for you, Nicky.

So —

The taxi's taken ten minutes to get here. I'll be late. Come with me, Suzie. You can stop me doing that sneaky Gavin Mellor a mischief!

Ha! Ha! I'm not sure I *WANT* to stop you — but okay!

Don't worry, miss. I know a short cut. I'll get you there on time!

I don't know this part of town.
Nicky! Look! It's *HER* — *LUCIE!* Stop the taxi!

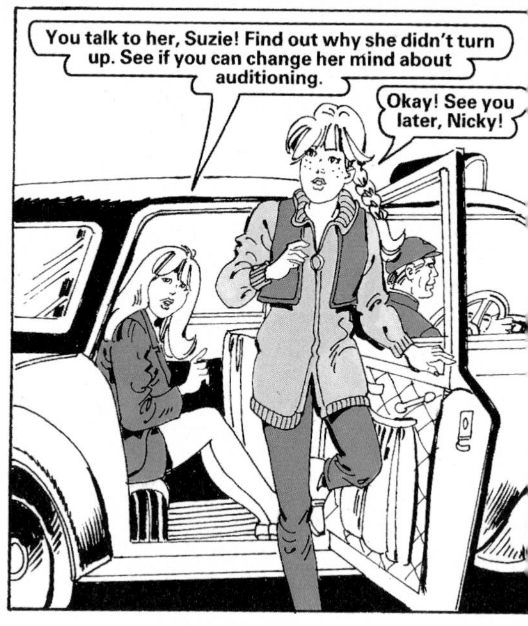

You talk to her, Suzie! Find out why she didn't turn up. See if you can change her mind about auditioning.
Okay! See you later, Nicky!

Crowds had gathered for the supermarket opening.
Nice try, ratbag. Your little trick *HELPED* me and Suzie sort out a problem. We couldn't have done it without you.
Tch! Nicky's got here after all!

Meanwhile —

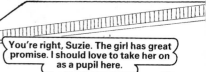

There was no point in coming to the audition, Suzie. My older brother and sister are at Uni — and Dad's building firm has just lost a big contract, so we're really skint, Suzie.

Your dad's a *BUILDER?* Lucie, I think I can see a way out of this! Please come with your dad to see Madame Celeste! *PLEASE!* Your talent can't go to waste!
Well . . . I . . . I . . . I'll try, Suzie!

You're right, Suzie. The girl has great promise. I should love to take her on as a pupil here.
The next day —

So that's arranged, Mr Hodges? You do the work needed at the theatre, for whatever the fundraising show raises and I'll take ucie on here. When your business picks up, you can pay Lucie's fees.
It's a deal, adame Celeste.
Dad! Thanks!
A few days later, the auditions for the show were held.
I reckon *I'LL* be chosen to dance one of the leads.
Jocasta's showing off again — but she could be in for a shock!
The lead dancers will be Daniel, Marilynn, David, and Lucie.
WH-WHAT?
Jocasta won't like being passed over. But it's something every erformer has to learn to live with.
But, later —
Lucie, well done for being picked.
Oh! Thanks, Jocasta!
Well! Good for Jocasta! That was nice of her. I think she's starting to change.
Looks like we'll be left with the bighead of the school. Think there's any chance of *HIM* ever changing?
Gavin? *NO WAY!* Ha! Ha! Ha!
THE END

PONY SURPRISE

JEN MARTIN *spent all her free time helping out at a local riding stables. One day —*

Well, that's the mucking-out finished. Now I can start grooming.

Hi, Jen.
Hi! Enjoy your ride?
It must be great having your own pony. Sue and Katie are so lucky.

A few days later —
Jen! Can you come here a moment? I've someone I want you to meet.
Sure, Sara.

This is Tempo — he's on approval. I'd like you to look after him until he settles down.
I'd love to.

You're a friendly boy.

Stand now, Tempo.
He's really easy to groom.

There — finished.
You've done a really good job. You can start riding him tomorrow.

so —
We'll just take things easy today. The countryside round here will be strange to you, and I don't want you getting upset.

He's taking everything in his stride. He's a real treat to ride.

er —
Well, how was he?
Great. I'll give him his feed before I go.

, next day —
Look at Tempo. He recognises you, Jen.
Isn't that sweet?

Shall we go for a canter today, boy?

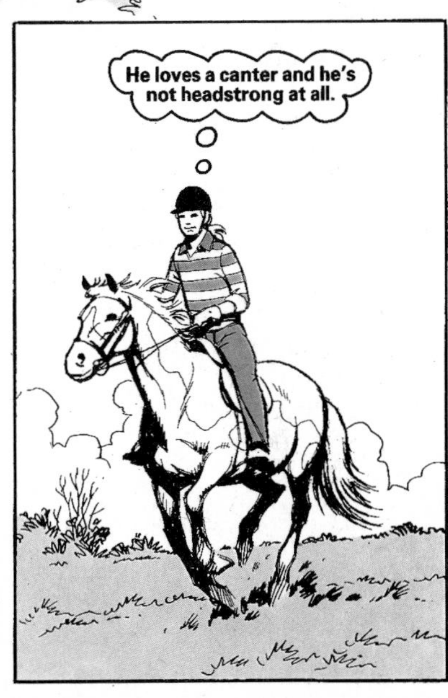
He loves a canter and he's not headstrong at all.

w days later —
Nearly done, Tempo, then perhaps we can go for another ride. You'll like that, won't you?

Jen, have you got a minute? I've got some news for you.
Sure,Sarah, what is it?

I'm afraid Tempo's been sold. The new owner will be taking over tomorrow.
What? Oh, no!

I suppose I knew this would happen one day. But I'll miss you, Tempo.

The next morning —
It's going to be hard to say goodbye. I've grown really fond of him.

But, later —
Surprise, surprise!
What? I can't believe it! Is he REALLY mine?
TO JENI FROM MUM + DAD

He's yours. Your parents wanted to make sure you'd take good care of a pony before they bought you one — and you've certainly proved that.
It's wonderful. I'm so happy.

You're mine, Tempo, an
I'll take good care fo you,
promise.

I couldn't be happier. I'm the luckiest girl in the whole world.
THE EN

All the gorgeous hunky guys listed are hidden in the grid. How quickly can you find them? Words can be read up, down, backwards, forwards or diagonally. Letters can be used more than once. This is a mega tricky challenge.

D E A N G A F F N E Y U I O S E V E E R U N A E K
T O B Y A N S T I S F R E D O R H C S K C I R T L
N I C K P I C K A R D R D A M O N A L B A R N T I
R T Y U Y L L E N N O D N A L C E D N H G U I I V
O O H U J H N B V D F D T Y U I R K A A V H J P C
D D S E R Y D A J H J T U H N I E G D N H G F D J
D A F S B N M O N J D M B N G J M I U T F D G A N
O V G I K J W A D O H G T N B V M R T M I A T R C
F I U U Y E W S R E A Y T A G H U E R C Y V L B E
R D E R S G M A E J N H I M B S R Z E P Y I E Z N
E D S C C H N P M O I K W M M G B Z T A E D E R C
T U L M J A S S I E C W E A S G R A T R V C S A J
A C L O O N G N T Y T D L E M I E L O T R H H A J
L H O T H N B E R L E E B N A G T O R L A O A L E
S O H B N U U W O A S Y T A D N E N T I H K R E W
N V C N N C O O M W T R T H A A I I E N N A P X C
A N I B Y R V K Y R O R E S T Y D T G S A C E J L
I Y N N D E H R N E N E R T T R H R R G I H E A F
T R L H E T R A O N I B B C E N B A O M R I H M A
S Y U T P E V M T C P K J H R P L M E F B I P E E
I U A H P P F G H E G C J K B G I F G E L L O S Y
R U P E R G D S E D A I R T I M I D X E L A F R F
H H K C R A I G Y O U N G H F T T I N I A V N K A
C U S T E V E G A T E L Y M N I A C N A E D T H G
L B H N I K M H N F F O H L E S S A H D I V A D C
J A A S O N S I M M O N S R E C N E P S E I S S E

A

B

C

D

CAN YOU NAME THE FOUR HUNKS PICTURED ABOVE?

TV HUNK

Answer the clues and place the FIRST letter of each answer in the shapes provided. If your answers are correct, the shaded letters will spell out the name of this gorgeous guy from Neighbours.

1. Colour of c
2. Birds lay th
3. Opposite of
4. Sixth month
5. Lazy
6. Planet and

GUYS PUZZLES

ANSWERS ON PAGE 112

'T ADAMS
ON ALBARN
N ALFORD
NE AMMANN
' ANSTIS
Y BARLOW
BERRY
'T BLEWITT
BON JOVI
ER BRUMMER
N CAIN
D CHOKACHI
CRUISE
ER CUNNAH
NNY DEPP
K DIMITRIADES
AN DONNELLY
D DUCHOVNY
T DORAN
FALZON
N GAFFNEY
VE GATELY
N GIGGS
AN HARVEY
ID HASSELHOF
K JAMES
S KEMP
Y LAWRENCE
TINO LAZZERI
N MAGUIRE
Y MORTIMER
McPARTLIN
L NICHOLLS
RK OWEN
E PERRY
I PETERS
K PICKARD
D PITT
NU REEVES
CE SAMAZAN
K SCHRODER
SHARPE
SON SIMMONS
ISTIAN SLATER
SIE SPENCER
TESTONI
RGE TROTTER
IG YOUNG

hoccie bar
Witch's pet
Short sleep
Crunchy fruit
Frozen water
Shape of circle

star initials

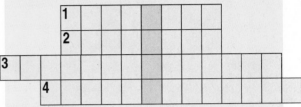

Answer the clues to find the star guys. If you're correct, the initials of their surnames, reading down, will spell out a word connected with Winter.

1. He plays Superman.
2. He used to be in Take That.
3. Grange Hill star.
4. 'X' File star.

STAR QUIZ

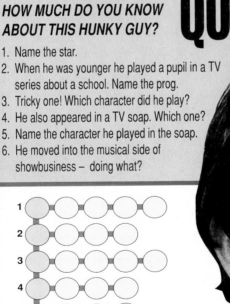

HOW MUCH DO YOU KNOW ABOUT THIS HUNKY GUY?

1. Name the star.
2. When he was younger he played a pupil in a TV series about a school. Name the prog.
3. Tricky one! Which character did he play?
4. He also appeared in a TV soap. Which one?
5. Name the character he played in the soap.
6. He moved into the musical side of showbusiness – doing what?

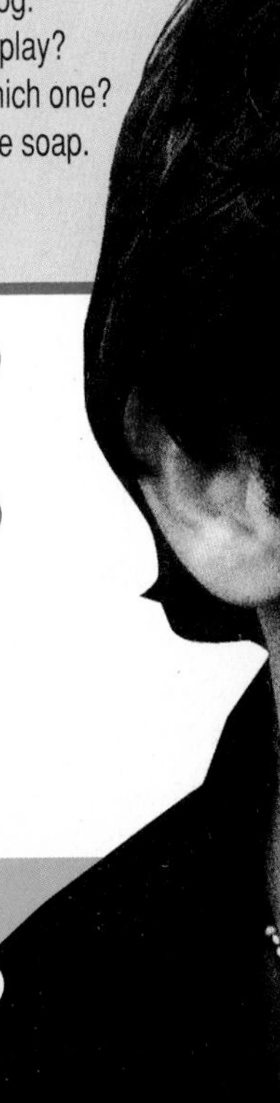

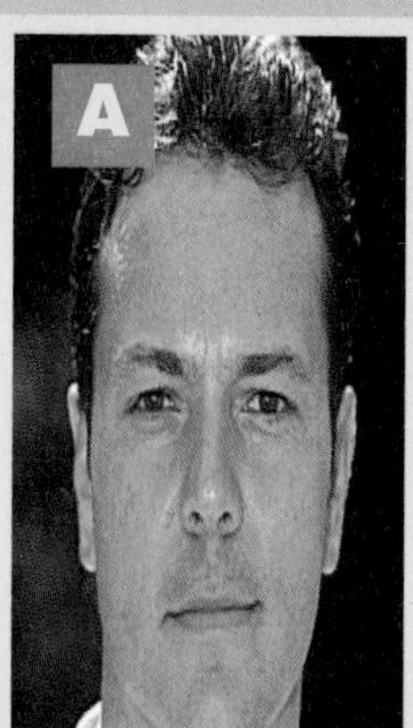

NAME THE GUYS

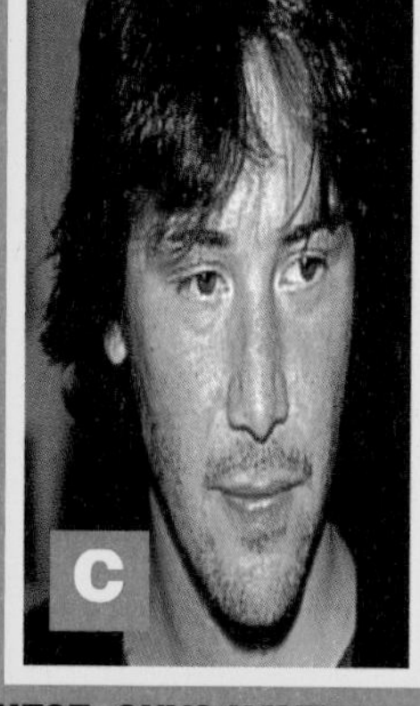

B

THESE GUYS HAVE GONE A BIT LONG IN THE FACE! WHO ARE THEY?

HUNKY GUYS PUZZLES

ANSWERS ON PAGE 112

POP PERSON

1. Unscramble the letters to give the name of this fave pop guy.
ARBIN YERAHV
2. Which group is he in?

WHO IS IT?

A) NAME THIS HUNKY GU
B) WHICH TOP TV PROG DOES HE APPEAR IN?
(As an added clue we've given you some of the letters of his name.)
D_V_D C_O_ _CH_

PAIRS

PAIR UP THE FIRST NAMES TO THE SURNAMES TO REVEAL FIVE FAVE GUYS.

HASSELLHOF
DAMON
AMALM
DONNELLY
ALBARN
GINOLA
DAVID
DAVID
DECLAN
DANIEL

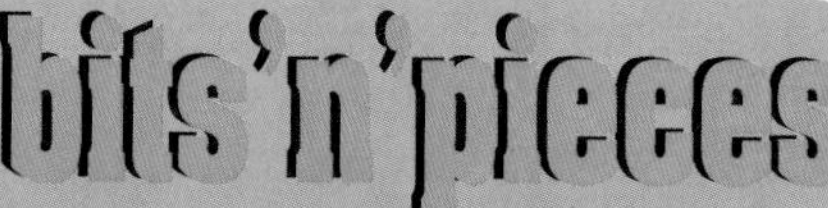

WHO IS THIS MEGA HUNK? HOW MANY TIMES DOES HE APPEAR?

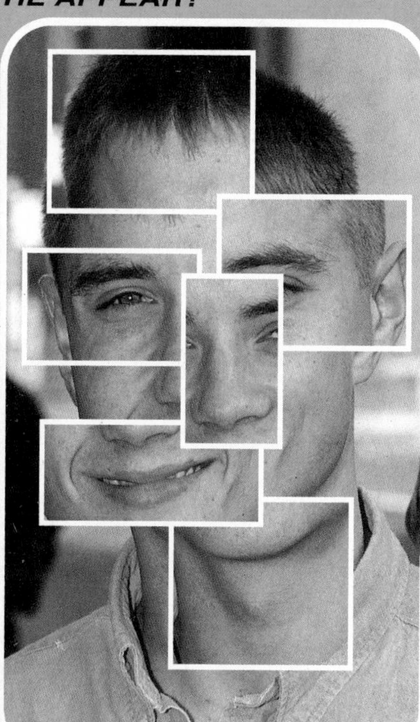

cross out

CROSS OUT THE LETTERS WHICH APPEAR THREE TIMES OR MORE TO LEAVE THE NAMES OF THESE TWO FAVE GROUPS, SHOWN BELOW.

C	J	O	M	L	Y
Y	K	T	C	T	W
W	A	W	K	L	J
T	J	M	Y	S	M
I	K	C	T	Y	C
L	J	M	K	L	S

A

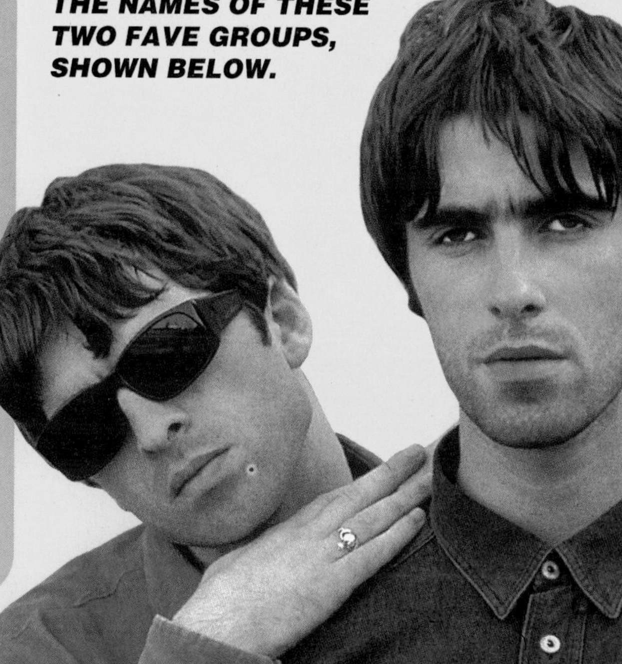

B

A	B	F	C	L	D
G	F	O	M	L	M
Y	M	G	F	Z	C
M	C	D	A	G	O
L	F	N	D	C	A
A	G	D	F	L	E

CRUNCHY

They're munchy! They're crunchy! In fact, apples are so good that most of us can't resist 'em! Here are a few recipe favourites of ours and yours!

APPLE DRINK

This one's great for long hot summer days or parties with friends.

Ingredients

2 lemons
2 oranges
1 cup water
50 g sugar
300 mls apple juice
ice cubes
600 mls soda water

Method

Cut two slices of lemon and orange from the fruit for decoration. Remove the skin from the rest of the fruit and place in a large jug with the rest of ingredients. Mix thoroughly. Decorate with slices of fruit and chill before serving.

CORN CRUNCH

Ingredients

3 dessert apples
50 g butter
50 g brown sugar
50 g golden syrup
100 g crushed cornflakes

Method

Peel, core and slice apples and place in a greased baking dish. Mix together all other ingredients and spread over apples. Bake for 20-25 minutes Gas Mark 5 /190°C/375°F. Serves 4.

EVE'S PUDDING

I'm the oldest in the 'M&J' office so I've chosen a very popular old-fashioned pudding. It's really yummy!

The Ed.

Ingredients

Base:
1 large cooking apple
25 g brown sugar
1 tablespoonful water

Topping:
50 g caster sugar
50 g margarine
1 egg (size 2-3)
50g self-raising flour

Method

Put oven on at Gas Mark 4/180°C/350°F.

Peel, core and slice apple. Place apple in small pan with water and brown sugar. Heat gently until apple is soft. Grease the oven-proof dish and spread apple mixture over base. Mix the margarine and caster sugar together. Beat the [egg] and add a little at a time with a little of flour. Add the rest o[f] the flour and fold it [in] gently. Spread the mixture over the to[p] of the apple. Bake [in] the oven for 35 minutes or until we[ll] risen and golden brown.

Serves two.

APPLE YOGHUR[T]

"This is my favourite breakfas[t]. I hope you enjoy i[t] too."

Caz

Ingredients

2 dessert apples
Juice of ½ lemon
1 small tub plain yoghurt
Clear honey

N' MUNCHY

thod

Core and peel ing apples and e them thinly into owl in which you e squeezed the non juice. Then, in other bowl, pour the yoghurt; mix three-quarters of the apple slices with this, reserving the remainder to decorate the top of the dish. Sprinkle clear honey and serve chilled.

Serves one.

BAKED APPLES

Ingredients

2 large cooking apples
25 g butter
50 g brown sugar
25 g sultanas or raisins

Method

Wash apples and remove cores, using an apple corer. Carefully cut a shallow slit through skin around middle of each apple. Stand the apples in a greased ovenproof dish. Fill the holes in the middle with brown sugar and sultanas. Add 2 tablespoonfuls water to the dish. Put a knob of butter on top of each apple. Bake at Gas Mark 4 /180°C/350°F for about 1 hour. Take care when removing the dish from the oven. Serve with custard.

Serves two.

Joyce Dalgety, Arbroath.

APPLE MUFFINS

Ingredients

1 cooking apple
225 g plain flour
Pinch of salt
2 rounded teaspoonfuls baking powder
50 g butter or margarine
50 g sugar
2 tablespoonfuls water

Method

Peel, core and chop the apple finely. Sieve the flour, salt and baking powder into a mixing bowl. Rub in the butter until the mixture resembles fine breadcrumbs. Add the sugar and chopped apple and mix to a soft dough with the water. Roll out to 1½ cm thickness and cut with a 5 cm cutter. Place the muffins on a lightly-greased baking sheet and bake in a moderate oven for 25-30 minutes. Gas Mark 4/180°C/350°F. Split while hot and spread with butter.

Jane Sanderson, Cardiff.

make 'n

It's dead annoying when your room's all messy and you can't find anything. It's even more annoying when the Olds are nagging you to tidy it! So, get everything in order with our brill storage solutions.

The storage boxes are made from old fruit boxes which are specially made to stack. They're very strong and they're FREE from supermarkets. You can usually find them at the checkouts, but if not, don't afraid to ask for some. Supermarkets are normall only too pleased to help. Try to get a few of the same boxes as they'll fit together best.

To decorate your boxes you'll need:

- Emulsion paint
- Pritt Stick
- Small pieces of tissue paper

We used paint from the Dulux Definitions range. You can choose from over a 1000 colours and have a 250ml matt emulsion sample (enough for 3-4 boxes) mixed for only £1.99.

Carefully remove any loose labels that are stuck to the boxes and then paint the outside. You may need 2 or 3 coats — let each coat dry before doing the next one. We left the inside of our boxes unpainted, but they look nice painted, too. Try mixing some white emulsion with your main colour to get a paler shade for the inside.

When the boxes are dry you can decorate them. We added flowers from torn pieces of tissue. Tear out petal shapes — they don't all need to be perfect — and glue them on with the Pritt. You'll need 6 petals and a centre for each flower.

Instead of using tissue, you could sponge on a painted design. You'll find instructions on how to do this on page 89.

Use your boxes to store all kinds of things — jumpers, shoes, socks 'n' tights, books, tapes and CDs, school stuff, mags or just about anything you like.

The matching storage pots are handy for hair accessories, pens 'n' pencils, cotton wool balls, jewellery and lots more. They're easy-peasy — all you need is some plain coloured paper, empty cardboard tubs (drinking chocolate and powdered milk come in these) and glue.

Cover the outside of the tubs by glueing on the coloured paper. Decorate the pots to match your boxes and fill 'em up! That's all there is to it.

UPSID

CHRIS LENG

GILES KRISTIAN

RICHARD MICALLEF

JAMIE BROWNE

JANUARY

MONDAY	–	6	13	20	27
TUESDAY	–	7	14	21	28
WEDNESDAY	1	8	15	22	29
THURSDAY	2	9	16	23	30
FRIDAY	3	10	17	24	31
SATURDAY	4	11	18	25	–
SUNDAY	5	12	19	26	–

FEBRUARY

MONDAY	–	3	10	17	24
TUESDAY	–	4	11	18	25
WEDNESDAY	–	5	12	19	26
THURSDAY	–	6	13	20	27
FRIDAY	–	7	14	21	28
SATURDAY	1	8	15	22	–
SUNDAY	2	9	16	23	–

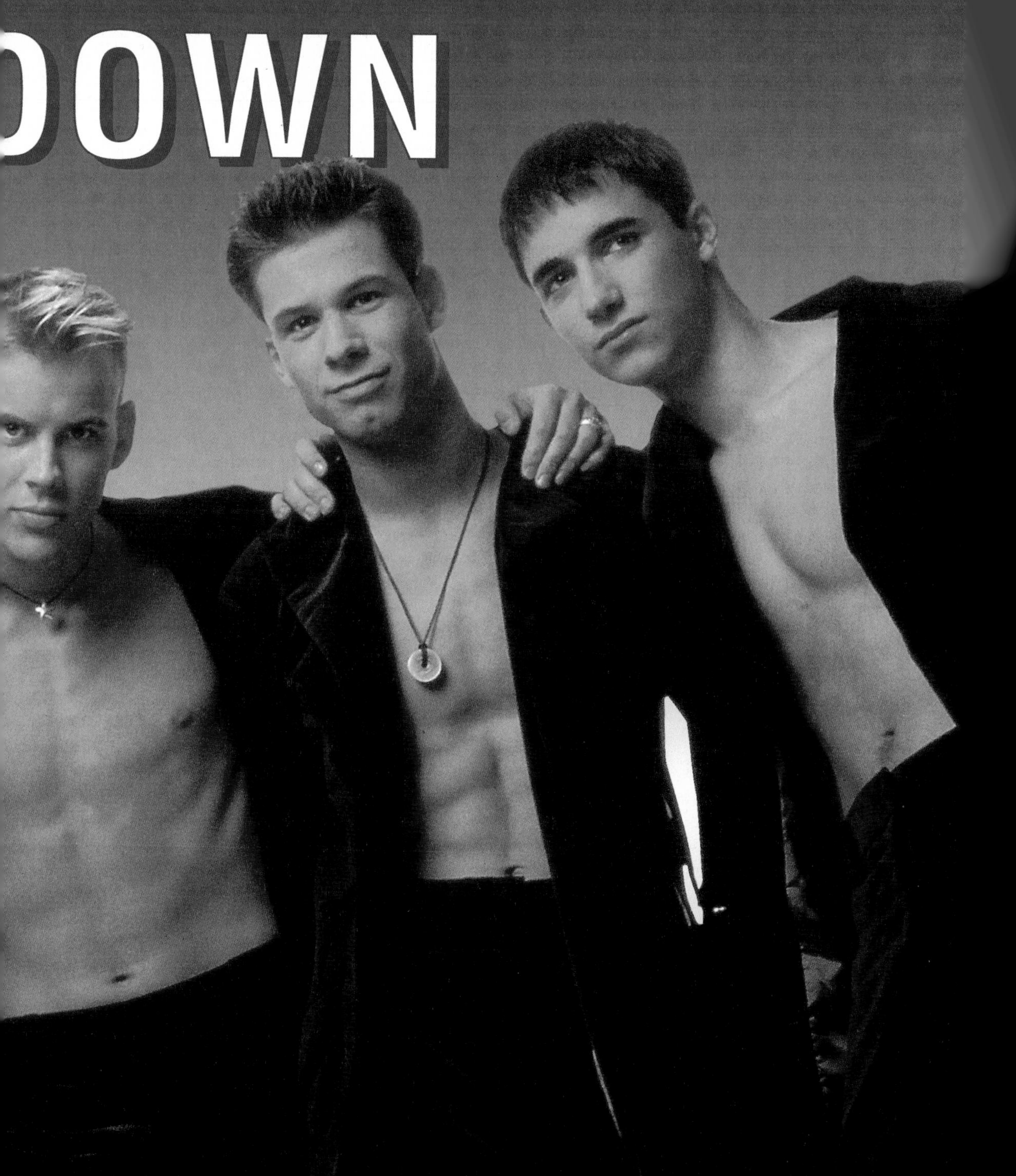

MARCH

ONDAY	–	3	10	17	24	31
ESDAY	–	4	11	18	25	–
EDNESDAY	–	5	12	19	26	–
URSDAY	–	6	13	20	27	–
IDAY	–	7	14	21	28	–
ATURDAY	1	8	15	22	29	–
NDAY	2	9	16	23	30	–

APRIL

MONDAY	–	7	14	21	28
TUESDAY	1	8	15	22	29
WEDNESDAY	2	9	16	23	30
THURSDAY	3	10	17	24	–
FRIDAY	4	11	18	25	–
SATURDAY	5	12	19	26	–
SUNDAY	6	13	20	27	–

funny FAX!

Jim Carrey's everyo

Check out this info . . .

- He comes from Canada.
- He's a wrinkly old 34.
- When he was 13, his family lived in a camper van, but now Jim earns mega millions and lives in a Hollywood swank mansion.
- Jim's the youngest of 4 children. He has 2 sisters and a brother.
- At school his nickname was Jimmy Gene the String Bean.
- When he checks into hotels, Jim uses the false name of Clint Genterment to avoid being mobbed by fans.
- He can dislocate his shoulder and flop it around behind his shoulder. Yuk!
- He once played a red furry alien called Wiploc.
- Jim was once married and has a daughter called Jane. He now dates actress Lauren Holly who starred in DUMB AND DUMBER with him.
- Jane can do great impressions of a dog barking and growling. Sounds just like her Dad!
- Jim used to work in a factory making fibreglass insulation. He also made picture frames.
- Although he's pretty skinny already, Jim had to lose nearly 2 stones to fit into his tight RIDDLER costume for BARMAN FOREVER.
- Jim loved the BATMAN show when he was young, but he wasn't allowed to watch it if he didn't wash for bed properly first.

- He likes mega wrinkly old singer FRANK SINATRA.
- Jim has 4 dogs and a pet
- ACE VENTURA WHEN NA CALLS made more money ir first 3 weeks than ACE VEN PET DETECTIVE made altog
- Although it looks like WHI NATURE CALLS was made i Africa, it was actually filmed Carolina and Texas, USA.
- One of Jim's dogs went missing and he had to hire a pet detective to find him. It c $100.
- Not everyone loves funny Jim. The original female sta WHEN NATURE CALLS, Georgiana Robertson, left af only ONE day.
- He once had a water skiin accident and was hit in the f by the tip of a ski. He says th what makes his face twist sc much!

nny fave and we've got all you need to know about him.

You can laugh-alonga-Jim in these films:

- ACE VENTURA PET DETECTIVE
- ACE VENTURA WHEN NATURE CALLS
- THE MASK
- DUMB AND DUMBER
- BATMAN FOREVER
- THE DEAD POOL (with crumbly Oscar-winning actor CLINT EASTWOOD)
- PEGGY SUE GOT MARRIED (with Oscar-winning actor NICHOLAS CAGE)
- EARTH GIRLS ARE EASY (with Oscar-winning actress GEENA DAVIS)

Look out for him in new film CABLE GUY.

This Is Me!

This is the page where YOU lot are the stars! Is YOUR piccy here? YOU could be famous.

Name — Georgina Humphreys
Age — 11
Lives — Hornchurch
Likes — Oasis and M Pec
Dislikes — Pineapple and peas
Ambition — To be an actress and ride on dolphi

This is a photo of me an my brother in America.

Name — Tammy Timms
Age — 12
Lives — Hatfield
Loves — Animals and my nan!
Dislikes — Spiders, cruelty to animals
Ambition — To be a vet

The picture is of me and my baby cousin, Lucy.

Name — Catherine Mailey
Age — 10
Lives — Ballyboe, Co. Donegal
Likes — Boyzone, Man United, Ryan Giggs and tr
Dislikes — East 17, Liver and Newcastle football clu
Hobbies — Reading, runr gymnastics and football
Ambition — To be a sing

P.S. This is a photo of m on my holidays in Major

Hi! My name's Caron. Here are some details about me:
Name — Caron Phillips
Age — 10
Lives — Mid Glamorgan, South Wales
Hobbies — Reading, karate, judo and swimming
Likes — East 17, MN8
Hates — Michael Jackson
Favourite food — Spaghetti Bolognaise
Favourite TV prog — Top of the Pops
Ambition — To have a black belt in karate

Name — Lucy Allen
Age — 8
Lives — Accrington
Fave food — Pot Noodles
Fave film — Pocahontas
Fave TV prog — Home And Away
Collects — Stickers, soaps
Family — Mum, Dad, pets
Ambition — To be a vet

I would like to tell you few things about myself
Name — Ellen Clarkson
Age — 11
Lives — Birmingham
Pets — Dog and 2 hamst
Likes — P.E.
Hates — Homework
Hobbies — Swimming, netball and rounders
Best friends — Emily, Hannah and Charlotte

The BRIDESMAID

I'M really looking forward to Saturday. It's going to be the happiest day of my life!

You see, I've wanted to be a bridesmaid for years — so I'm thrilled to be getting my chance at last!

There was a time, a couple of years ago, when I thought I'd be bridesmaid to my cousin, Anne. She came round to our house, on the day she got engaged, to show us her ring and ask if I'd be her attendant. I was thrilled! I was so excited! I thought of nothing else for weeks!

I suppose that's why I didn't notice how bad things were getting between Mum and Dad. They kept having huge rows over something or other all the

The BRIDESMAID

time. If I hadn't been so wrapped up in the thought of being a bridesmaid, I'd probably have been worried about them. As it was, I didn't take much notice until it was too late. I arrived home from school one day and Mum told me Dad had left!

It was for good. He'd taken all his belongings. Yes, Dad had left — and with him had gone my chance of being a bridesmaid.

YOU see, Anne was DAD'S niece. So, when he left Mum and me, Anne decided she didn't want me as her bridesmaid after all. Mum and I weren't even invited to the wedding. I was devastated!

I suppose that was the least of my problems, though. Mum and I had to get used to life without Dad. He wanted a clean break it seemed, so he didn't even contact me. I never saw him any more — and that hurt!

It used to make me really sad when girls at school moaned about their dads making them tidy their bedrooms, or not letting them stay out late, or insisting they did their homework before they watched TV. I just wished I still had a dad to lay down rules — because then I'd have a dad to share the fun things with, too. They didn't know how lucky they were!

Money was tight as well. Mum went out and found a job, but we still weren't as well off as we'd been before. It got to the stage where I was almost afraid to ask for new clothes because I hated to see the worried expression on Mum's face.

I've got some new gear for Saturday, though!

"This is a special occasion," Mum told me happily. "You can have exactly what you like — never mind the expense."

It was so exciting looking at the dresses. The materials were gorgeous — and the colours were brilliant!

The dress I chose was covered in lovely pastel shaded flowers.

"It's beautiful!" Mum said. "But you'll need shoes as well, and a hat of some kind."

THE assistant scurried abo bringing differe accessories for me to try. I like a princess! In the end, bought flat pumps — alm like ballet shoes — and a cre coloured straw hat. Then I tr on the whole lot and looked the mirror.

"You look lovely!" M breathed.

Gran and Auntie Be nodded. I had to admit I w thrilled when I saw r reflection. I've never thought myself as pretty, but I looke in my bridesmaid's clothes!

"You'll outshine the brid Mum continued, laughing.

I turned from the mirror.

"No, Mum. I could ne outshine *you*," I told her firm "You'll be a fantastic bride and Malcolm will make a sup dad."

That's why I'm looki forward to Saturday so mu Not only am I going to be bridesmaid for the first time my life, but, when Mum g married again, I'll have a n dad — a really nice dad, to like Malcolm a lot and we on well.

Yes, as I said, Saturday going to be the happiest day my life!

THE END

copy kat

IT was Friday and thirteen-year-old Rachel Mason was leaving school with her friend, Janie.

Hurry up, Janie. I want to go to the paper shop for my mag. I didn't have time to get it this morning.
Coming, Rachel.

A few minutes later —

Let's see what Kat's up to this week. She's my fave character.

Look! She's researching a story for the school mag and she unearths something interesting and gets it printed in the local newspaper. *WOW!*
I wish I could be like her!

The story *I* had to do for the school mag a few weeks ago was *SO-OO* boring, but look at what Kat does! It's really exciting!
Hey, it's only a story, Rachel! Don't take it *TOO* seriously! Anyway, I'm off now! See you tomorrow!

Soon —

Hello, Rachel. Had a good day? What have you been up to?
Usual stuff, Harriet. You know — school work, beating the boys to the best table for lunch . . .
Harriet's a great neighbour. She's always really interested in me. Strange — cos I always think I sound dull. Harriet would love talking to Kat, that's for sure!

Later, at the local library —
Hello, Rachel. What are you up to this weekend, then? Anything interesting?
Oh, hi, Harriet. I'm not sure what I'm doing.
SPONSORED ROLLATHON Saturday 2p.m.
What would Kat say if Harriet asked her? It's the sponsored rollathon tomorrow. Kat would be sure to take part in that. Hey, why don't I be like Kat then and enter?
So —
I think I'll take part in the rollathon.
I'll sponsor you, Rachel.
There! That was an easy decision.
But, later —
I must be *CRAZY!* I'll have to borrow my cousin Pat's skates, get some sponsors and practise. I've *NEVER* roller-skated before!
WENDY
So, the following morning —
I've lost count of how many times I've fallen. I'm hopeless!

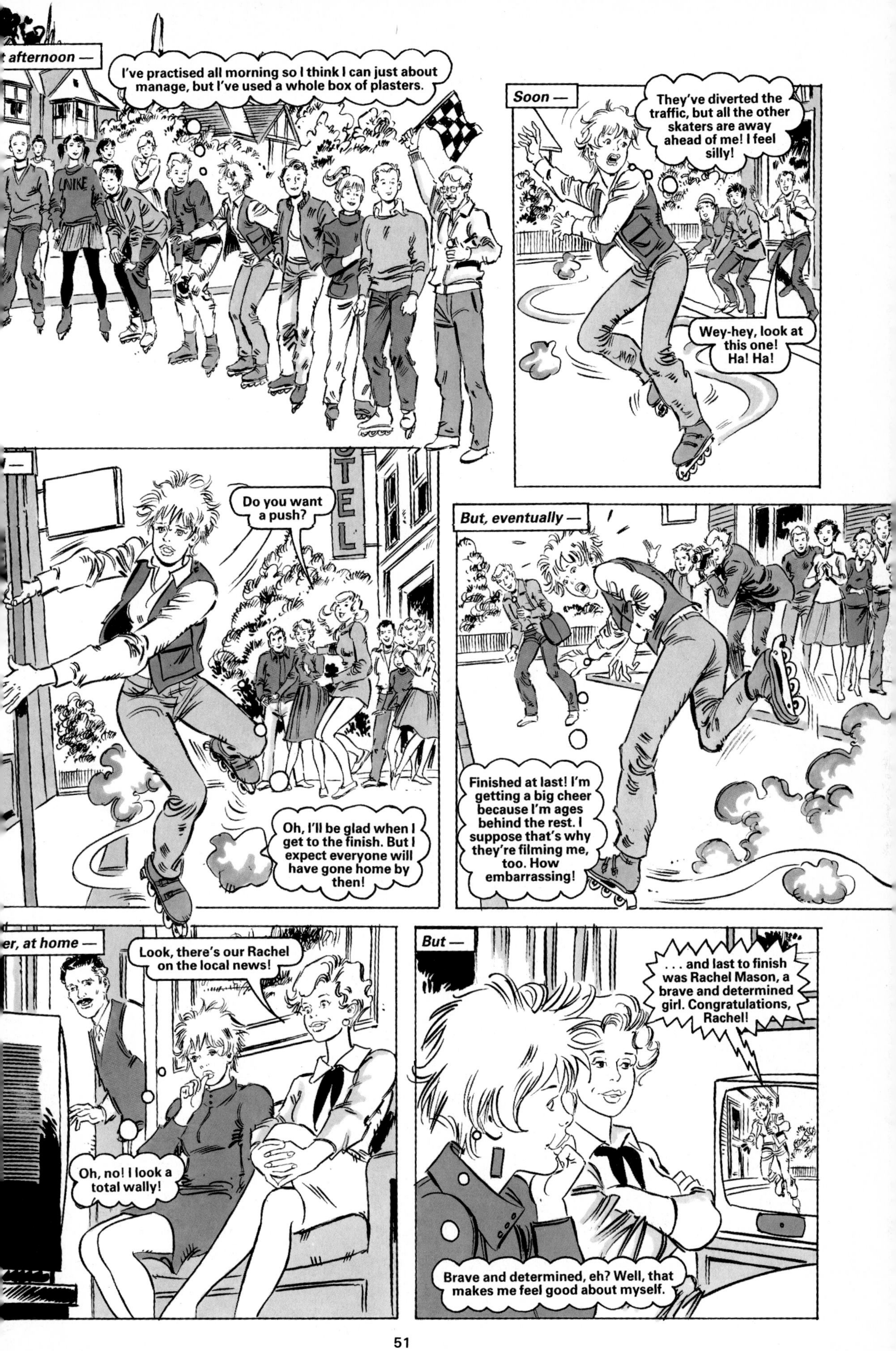

t afternoon —

I've practised all morning so I think I can just about manage, but I've used a whole box of plasters.

Soon —

They've diverted the traffic, but all the other skaters are away ahead of me! I feel silly!

Wey-hey, look at this one! Ha! Ha!

Do you want a push?

Oh, I'll be glad when I get to the finish. But I expect everyone will have gone home by then!

But, eventually —

Finished at last! I'm getting a big cheer because I'm ages behind the rest. I suppose that's why they're filming me, too. How embarrassing!

er, at home —

Look, there's our Rachel on the local news!

Oh, no! I look a total wally!

Next day —
Saw you on the local news last night, Rachel. Well done! Come and tell me all about it.
Okay, Harriet.
My story won't be as exciting as Kat's would be. She would have been first past the finish in record time! Still, I enjoy chatting to Harriet.

Then, on Monday —
Rachel, it's late. Stop reading and come down this minute!
Oh! Right, Mum.
I lost track of the time. I wanted to remind myself of all the things Kat's been doing over the past few weeks. I'll hardly have time for breakfast.

Soon —
You're full of energy as usual, Rachel.
ENERGY? I feel worn out already! Trust Harriet to see it like that. Really I'm just worried about being late.

At break —
I didn't know you were taking part in the rollathon on Saturday, Rachel.
We saw you. We were in the crowd. You were a hoot, Rachel.

It was great to see you on the local news though, Rachel. They called you brave and determined.
Brilliant!
She was!

to Rachel. Anyone there? Rachel,
've been talking to you and I
n't think you've heard a word.
Oh! Sorry, Janie. I was . . . er . . . thinking.
About Kat.

I want to know what's going on over there — see?
Okay — come on then, Janie.

There's something moving high up in the tree. We think the janitor's new kitten's stuck.
Kat would have that kitten rescued in no time. Hey! If Kat would do it, then *I* can! Here goes!

This is hard
nd . . . rats! I've
pped my skirt!

Where? *AAH!* I'm falling!
There it is! I saw the leaves move!

Continued on Page 97

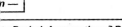

The problem is...

waiting ...
Last time I went to hospital I had to wait HOURS..
Pete always spoils things for me... I can't miss this party...
But mum's taking me to a party... it starts soon....
Hurry up mum!
... waiting....
oooh... now that's INTERESTING...
£10
PRING TAXIS tel: 6951147
AND WAITING. ...
could just call a taxi... Mum knows how much I want to go... She wouldn't mind. She'll pay the money back...
PRING TAXIS Tel.....
suddenly...
BBRIINGG
Brriingg
ring
recall
redial
secrecy
Pete needs a plaster cast and we'll be here a while... So Dad is coming to pick you up and take you to the party...
thanks, Mum!
I nearly did something VERY WRONG there... Ordering a taxi and taking money to pay for it is well out of order. Good job Mum phoned when she did...
... honesty really IS the best policy.

Who Needs

**Everyone needs friends! But how good a mate are you
Try our quiz and find out . . .**

1. IN THE SCHOOL PLAYGROUND YOU OVERHEAR SOME PEEPS SAYING SOMETHING VERY NASTY ABOUT YOUR BEST MATE. DO YOU:

b. Join in the chat!
a. Listen in, then tell your friend EVERYTHING you'd heard said.
c. Try not to listen — you and your mates probably talk about them sometimes, so it's not worth bothering about.
d. March up to them in a temper and tell them exactly what you think of them.

2. YOUR BEST MATE'S GUY HAS JUST GIVEN HER THE BIG E. SHE'S DEVASTATED AND COMES ROUND TO YOUR HOUSE. DO YOU —

a. Tell her to cheer up — he wasn't very nice anyway!
b. Ask her to stop whining — everyone loses a boyfriend sometime.
c. Make her a cuppa and listen to her — it'll do her good to talk things over.
d. Take her to the nearest disco — well, the sooner she finds a new guy the better!

3. A GUY YOUR FRIEND HAS FANCIED FOR AGES ASKS YOU OUT. DO YOU —

c. Refuse — tell him you're going out with someone else.
a. Go on a date with him, regret it at once and have the miseries for weeks.
b. Go out with him — all's fair in lurve, isn't it?
d. Tell him no way — but mention that you know a girl who really fancies him and would love to.

4. YOUR BEST MATE'S BOUGHT NEW GEAR. YOU THINK SHE LOOKS THE PITS IN IT. SHE ASKS YOU WHAT YOU THINK. DO YOU:

a. Waffle and say that the colour suits her . . . the material's nice . . . the gear will wear well . . .
b. Say you've seen smarter scarecrows! What on earth was she thinking c when she bought the clothes?
c. Tell her it suits her, though yo seen her look better. You're think to yourself that she'll soon outgr the gear.

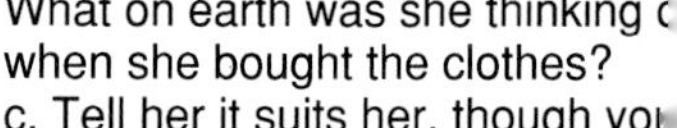

d. Suggest going back to the sho to buy MORE gear with the cash has left, hoping that she'll take yo opinions into account this time.

5. YOU AND YOUR MATE HAV BEEN INVITED TO A PARTY. THAT GUY YOU FANCY WILL THERE. IT'S GOING TO BE FANTASTIC. THEN YOUR MAT ANNOUNCES THAT SHE HAS BABY-SIT FOR HER AUNTIE A WANTS YOU TO COME TOO. D YOU:

d. Go for a while then take over t baby-sitting and let her go to the party.
a. Go to the party but don't enjoy because you think you should ha gone baby-sitting.
c. Go baby-sitting with her.
b. Go, have a good time, and nex day tell your friend all about it an about how great it was.

6. YOUR MATE'S LATE FOR SCHOOL FOR THE THIRD TIM A WEEK. TEACHER ASKS YOU WHERE SHE IS. DO YOU:

a. Say you don't really know, but could be chatting up John from c Two A.
c. Explain that she's slept in agai because she hasn't been getting lot of sleep with toothache.
b. Remark she's lazy and doesn't

Mates?

ɘ getting up in the morning.
Suggest that she's been cornered the street by a tiger that's caped.

YOUR BEST FRIEND LENT YOU R NEW TOP TO GO TO A SCO. YOU SPILT DOWN IT AND S RUINED. DO YOU:

c. Explain exactly what happened and promise to buy her a new one next time you have some dosh.
d. Tell her it has a stain on it and that it's in the wash. (You're hoping the dry cleaner's will achieve what you couldn't.)
b. Laugh hysterically when you tell her about her top and y it could have been worse — it 't torn and she can replace it ıen she gets some birthday cash.
Keep forgetting to return the top ping that she'll eventually give up king for it back.

8. YOU SEE YOUR MATE'S GUY IN TOWN, HAND IN HAND WITH ANOTHER GIRL. DO YOU:

a. Tell her straight out.
b. Forget it and do nothing — he's HER boyfriend.
c. Speak to the guy and ask him what's going on. Then tell him to make sure to speak to your friend about it.
d. Tell the other girl exactly what you think of her in no uncertain terms.

9. YOUR MATE'S EXPECTING YOU FOR TEA. AT THE LAST MINUTE A GUY YOU LIKE A LOT ASKS YOU OUT. DO YOU:

d. Phone her with an over-the-top excuse.
c. Try to change the date to another day and go for tea.
a. Go to her place for half an hour but make an excuse not to stay for tea.
b. Phone her and tell her you're not coming. Something better's turned up.

10. YOUR MATE ASKS YOU TO LOOK AFTER HER GRAN'S DOG FOR A DAY. YOU HATE THE DISOBEDIENT BAD-TEMPERED LITTLE ANIMAL. DO YOU:

a. Say that you'll only do it if she bribes you with something great.
c. Agree, but remind yourself to keep him on the lead all the time.
b. Tell her, no way! You'd rather look after a gorilla for a fortnight!
d. Say that you'll do it intending to bribe someone else to walk the little pest.

CONCLUSIONS

Mostly a's

You do try, but sometimes you could do with being a bit more tactful. You'd be put out if your mate said some of the things you say to her. Not everyone likes to hear the absolute truth all the time. Maybe it would be better to say zilch than to upset your mate. There's nothing wrong in saying what you think, but don't overdo it!

Mostly b's

Your mate has feelings, you know, and you really need to do some thinking about how you treat people. You can't go through life tramping on peeps. Carry on like you are and you'll lose your mate. Treat her with some more respect. After all, you'd expect the same from her!

Mostly c's

You're a real friend. You'll stick by your mate through anything. She'll always be able to trust you.

There's one little prob, though. You're so easy to get on with and so nice to know that it would be very easy to take a loan of you. Make sure that your best mate thinks as much of you as you do of her!

Mostly d's

You're always cheerful and cracking jokes. Chances are you drive your mate crazy! Sometimes you'll be a bit too much to handle. Not a lot of peeps can be as optimistic as you.

You're a good mate, but you go a bit too far with your schemes sometimes. Have a good think before acting. You'll get on a lot better — and so will your mate.

nurses

AMANDA, Verity, Jackie and Kay were nursing students at Norchester General Hospital and shared a house. One evening, a week before Christmas —
What are we going to do for Christmas dinner?
I don't fancy cooking a turkey and all the trimmings.
Nor me! How about going out for a meal instead?
That'll be dead expensive.
I know, but it IS Christmas. We deserve a treat! Let's go to The Riverside Hotel! It's nice there.
We'll need to reserve a table. I'll do it now. I hope they're not fully booked.
The number's engaged. I'll try again later.
Okay. We'd better do some studying now. Exams in the New Year!
But, a short time later —
It's the hospital! There's been a pile-up on the motorway. All available staff are to report to casualty. Let's go!
Soon —
The Andrews' car was crushed by a lorry. I don't know if they'll pull through. We're transferring Mr Andrews to intensive care. His wife's already there.

There's a little girl in my cubicle — Emma Andrews. It must be her parents you've just sent up to intensive care, Amanda.
XRAY
She's not badly hurt. She was in the back of the car. You're working on children's ward this week, aren't you? Would you have a word with Emma, Amanda?
No prob, Kay!
Hello, Emma! My name's Nurse Bailey. I'm going to be looking after you on the ward.
Will you look after Tiny, too?
ny's her bear. She n't let go of it since e was brought in.
Of course I will. Nurse Baxter is going to take you upstairs to the children's ward now your leg's been plastered. I'll see you there in the morning when you wake up.
All right.
e next day —
I've brought you breakfast, Emma.
Thank you. Are there corn flakes? Tiny likes cornflakes.
Yes — we'll sit Tiny on the tray and he can tuck in, too.

That girl certainly loves her teddy.
Her parents are seriously ill in intensive care. The bear's her only comfort at the moment.
Meanwhile, in the nurses' canteen —
What are you up to, Gary?
I'm cooking the turkey meal in our flat and I don't want to forget anything!
Let's see — stuffing, bread sauce, cranberry sauce, gravy, sprouts . . .
Sounds too much like hard work to me! We've decided to go out for our meal.
A few days later —
Three cheers for the hospital porters, children! They've decorated the tree beautifully.
It's lovely!
Glad you all like it!
We certainly do! And now, children, we're going to do something else to decorate the ward for Christmas.
All of you who are out of bed, come to the day room with me. We're going to make paper chains!

What's wrong, Emma?
It's Tiny! He's *GONE!*
Don't cry! I expect he's just fallen on the floor. I'll have a look.
But—
I can't see him. Maybe one of the other children has put him in the toy box by mistake.
Rats! I can't see Tiny here either.
What's up?
Emma's lost Tiny.
She'll be heart-broken. I hope he turns up.
TOY BOX

But he didn't. Next day —
Emma hasn't eaten any lunch, sister.
It's because of that missing bear. It could set back her recovery.
We need to do something to take h mind off Tiny. Maybe a visit to her parents! I could push Emma in a wheelchair.
Out of the question! They're still in intensive care. Seeing them surrounded by tubes and equipment might upset her even more.

After work —
I've had another idea. This bear looks *ALMOST* like Tiny to me. He's wearing a Father Christmas suit, but, if I take that off, I'm sure Gemma will never notice the difference.
GIFTS
That's two pounds fifty, please.
Santa Ted

The next day —
Emma won't eat and she won't talk. I'm very worried about her.
It's all right, sister! I think I've solved the problem!

Look, Emma! I've found Tiny!

That's not Tiny. He's not the right colour. Tiny's a darker brown than that!
Huh! It's only a slight difference. I'm amazed she noticed!
Later —
So much for your idea. NOW what?
It's Christmas Day tomorrow. Gemma will be given gifts by the Hospital Friends' Association. That could help to take her mind off Tiny.
But, on Christmas morning —
Are you watching, children? I'm going to hang up the paper chains you made now.
Gemma's hardly looked at her gifts. Doctor's really worried about her.
Careful, Jackie! You've knocked the fairy off the tree. I'll put it back.
There we are! Oh!
It's TINY!

Look what I've found, Emma! One of the porters must have found him on the floor, thought he was a decoration, and tied him on to the tree.
TINY!

Emma's happy again — and I've just had word from intensive care. Her parents are finally out of danger.
That's great! It's going to be a happy Christmas for all of them!

When the girls finished duty —
We're home, Verity! What time is the table booked for?
Er . . . sorry, guys. I suddenly remembered this morning that I forgot to arrange it.

Oh, no! The restaurant will be full now.
I know. But I wasn't working this morning, so I've cooked instead.
Great! Turkey and Christmas pudding?

Not exactly — I didn't have the ingredients. So our Christmas dinner is made up of things we had in the freezer . . . curry or pizza, everyone?
I don't BELIEVE it! Oh well, this is one Christmas dinner we WON'T forget in a hurr
THE EN

The Ghost

SALLY MASON was keen on walking in the country. One day —
I'll go up Black Fell today. It's really nice there.
Just then —
Hi! Do you want to come with us?
That depends. Where are you going?
Sheep Crag.
Then no thanks. I want to walk up Black Fell.
What? You shouldn't go there on your own!
Why not?

It's supposed to be haunted!
Is that all? I'm not afraid of ghosts! A story like that won't put me off.
See you later!
Okay.
If the ghost doesn't get her!
Soon —
It's lovely up here — not spooky at all.
Then —
Oh! There's a mist coming down.
It's getting really thick. I can't see a thing.

HELP! I'M LOST!
I don't know why I'm calling. I'm sure there's nobody else up here.
But —
Hi!
Oh! Where did YOU come from?
Further up the hill. The mist doesn't bother me. I know this fell like the back of my hand.
I'll take you down.
Thanks!
This way.
She's really experienced.

At last —
Here we are! Back down safely, out of the mist.
Thank goodness.

There's those girls I saw earlier.

Are you okay? You look a bit shaken.

I got stuck in a mist. Luckily this girl turned up and led me down.

What girl?

She's over there. Oh! That's strange. She's gone!

I bet she was a ghost!

The ghost is supposed to be a girl. Apparently she fell and died while walking here some years ago.

See? We *TOLD* you the place was haunted — but *YOU* wouldn't believe us.
I didn't say I didn't believe them. I just said I wasn't afraid of ghosts — and I'm not.
Well . . . I'd better go.

But I do believe the fell's haunted. In fact, I *KNOW* it is!
The ghost isn't that girl who led me down, though. She was just a friendly walker.

The ghost of Black Fell is me!
THE END

dreams

ONE evening, Cassie was dreaming — not of a white Christmas — but of a possible day off school!
The weather forecast said heavy snow tonight. I hope it's right! We may not have to go to school tomorrow.
Sure enough —
Wow! Deep snow. Fantastic!
Because of the extreme weather, all schools in the area will remain closed today.
YES!

Will you clear all the snow off the drive before it freezes, Cassie, please?
Okay, Dad. I enjoy helping.
Well, actually, you'll be doing it on your own, Cassie. I'm afraid I'm going to work.
Oh!
So —
Phew! This is exhausting!
Finished at last. I'm going inside for a hot drink. My toes are frozen.
M'mm! That's better.
Cassie! I need your help.

Will you come to the supermarket with me?
Okay. I'll put on some dry socks while you get the car out of the garage.
I'm not driving in this weather! We'll have to walk. That's why I need your help.
Oh, no!
Later —
I never realised shopping could be so heavy. My arms are breaking! And my toes are frozen. *AGAIN!*
Never mind. It's not too far.
But, at home —
We'll soon warm up. Oh! What's happened? The radiators are cold!
The boiler's out. It must have broken. I'd better ring an engineer.

What did he say?
They're rushed off their feet in the cold snap. He can't come until tomorrow.
But the house is freezing! Haven't we any electric heaters?
No. There's just the open fireplace.
We'll just have to light a fire.
With what? We don't have any coal.
I know! You go to the common and collect some bits of firewood.
Aw, Mum!
So —
Some holiday from school this has turned out to be! It's been work, work, work all day. And my toes are nearly falling off!

At last —
That's the fire started.
Good! I can relax in the warm at last. Phew! My eyes are tired.

The next thing Cassie knew —
CASSIE! CASSIE! Wake up!
Uh?

Time to get up, Cassie. Look! The weather forecast was right last night. It has snowed!
I know that! Oh! It must have been a dream . . . well, more of a nightmare, actually. All that shovelling snow, going shopping and collecting firewood.

Which means the news about school being closed was just a dream, too. Rats! I bet they stay open.

But —
Your school's closed. They've just announced it on the radio.
Great! Er . . . do you want me to shovel snow now?

No! I did it before you got up.
What about you, Mum? Do you need me to go shopping?
No. We've a freezer full of food.
And the radiators are red hot, so I won't have to collect any firewood either. Ace! I can go out and have fun!
Soon —
Catch!
AAH!
Here we go!
This is great! My *REAL* day off school has turned out a lot better than my dream one did!
THE END

The Lucky Horseshoe

YOUNG Kirsty McDonald lived on an isolated farm in the Scottish Highlands. Her great companion was her pony, Robbie.
I love riding in the hills with you, Robbie!
On the way home —
Come on, Robbie! Let's jump the gate!

Oh, you've hit it!

A few minutes later —
Hello, Kirsty. I decided to give Robbie's stable a fresh coat of paint. It makes this old horseshoe look a bit shabby, although it never seems to rust.
I'll polish it! The fairy who left it there will be pleased, Dad.

That old story! Do you still believe a fairy came here asking for food for herself and her horse, and left one of its lucky shoes in return?
She promised it would save Corrie Farm one day. It's a lovely story, Dad, and I've always looked after the fairy shoe. Who knows? It might be true!

Later —
The horseshoe's shining again! Whatever Dad says, I do sort of believe the story.

A few days later —
There's a storm coming, Robbie. We'd better get home quickly.

re long, the storm broke.
What a wind! It's just as well you don't scare easily.

Suddenly, Robbie stumbled.
Careful, Robbie! Are you okay?

You've lost a shoe! You'll feel sore without it. Never mind — we haven't much further to go.

y made it safely home.
Kirsty! Thank goodness! The forecast's for severe gales. Get Robbie into the stable, then we'll make everything secure for the night.

A few hours later —
That crash was the barn door breaking open. I'll have to go out and fasten it!
We'll come and give you a hand, Ken.

Push! The door's nearly in place!
Mum . . . LOOK OUT!

She . . . she's badly hurt, Kirsty. Phone for an ambulance!
The telephone wires are own! I can ride for help . . . xcept . . . I forgot! Robbie lost a shoe, Dad!

Then, suddenly —
The fairy shoe seems to be glowing! I must be imagining it, but it could be the answer. Dad could fit the shoe to Robbie.

It's a wild idea, Kirsty, but old Robbie's safe and sensible, and your mum needs help quickly.

They set off into the storm.
We've got to jump that, Robbie. It's the only way out of our glen. I know you're not a great jumper, but try!

We're over! Well done, Robbi
But now we've to cross the fo
It will be flowing fast.

But Robbie was equal to the challenge.
Go on, Robbie! Good boy!

A bit further on —
There's been a landslide! It swept part of the track int the ravine. We've got to find way round, Robbie . . . and the only way is over the wa

And —
We're over! Robbie, you're wonderful! Now a straight gallop downhill into the village — and help!

And, a little later —
The wind's dropped enough for the helicopter to get to your mum. They'll have her safe in hospital very soon now.
Thanks to Robbie. Tonight something extra seemed to be helping him. Could it have been the fairy shoe?

A few days later —
Well, Kirsty, your mum's recovering, thanks to you and Robbie. The story about the fairy shoe might have some truth in it after all!
I'm sure of it, Dad. I've put the lucky horseshoe back on the stable. Who knows when we might need its help again?
THE EN

The problem is...

OH NO! looks like they've come to get megan WHAT SHOULD I DO?!
monitor
Too late ... They find her!
WE WANT A WORD WITH YOU
GULP
Yeh- about JANE
Then suddenly ...
AND I WANT A WORD WITH YOU
OUT!
I hope they don't find out it was ME...
opps
humpf
LATER...
Right, megan, I think you...
have some EXPLAINING to do...
You did the right thing in coming to me, kerry. And no one will know. You're doing a fine job as monitor, but some things are best left to me. WELL DONE!
thanks, miss

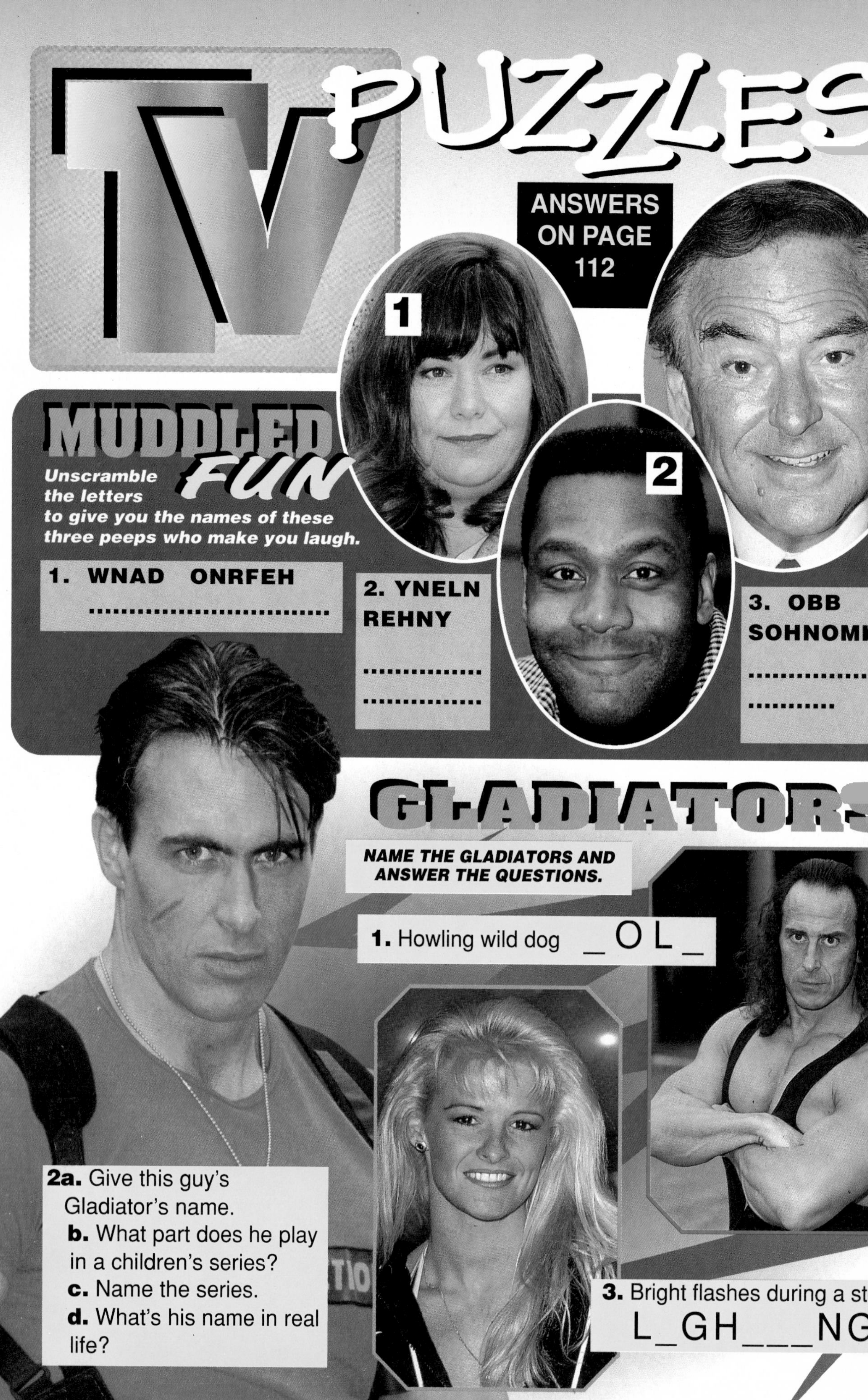

TV PUZZLES

ANSWERS ON PAGE 112

MUDDLED FUN

Unscramble the letters to give you the names of these three peeps who make you laugh.

1. WNAD ONRFEH ....

2. YNELN REHNY ....

3. OBB SOHNOM[…] ....

GLADIATORS

NAME THE GLADIATORS AND ANSWER THE QUESTIONS.

1. Howling wild dog _ O L _

2a. Give this guy's Gladiator's name.
b. What part does he play in a children's series?
c. Name the series.
d. What's his name in real life?

3. Bright flashes during a st[…]
L _ GH _ _ _ NG

soap time

. a) Name this star.
What soap
)es she appear in?
Which character
)es she play?

. Fill in the blanks to give this
unky guy's name and name
e soap he appears in.

_ C T _ S T O _ I
O _ E A _ _ A _ _ Y

3. a) Unscramble the letters to give the name of the person this guy plays in Neighbours.

S M A Z T A R K

b) What's his real name?

4. This actress appears in EastEnders.

a) Name her and the character she plays.

b) Name the guy who plays her brother, Robbie.

TELLY TEST

SO YOU'RE SQUARE EYED? WELL GIVE YOURSELF A MINUTE TO ANSWER THESE QUESTIONS ON TV PROGS.

1. In Casualty, what's Charlie's second name?
2. Name BBC's chart show.
3. Who presents Big Breakfast?
4. Which soap did the male presenter appear in and what part did he play?
5. Name the Saturday morning show the female presenter used to appear in.

Stars in their eyes

Try spotting these TV stars with stars in their eyes. You've one minute to come up with who they are:

TV PUZZLES

ANSWERS ON PAGE 112

TV PUZZLERS

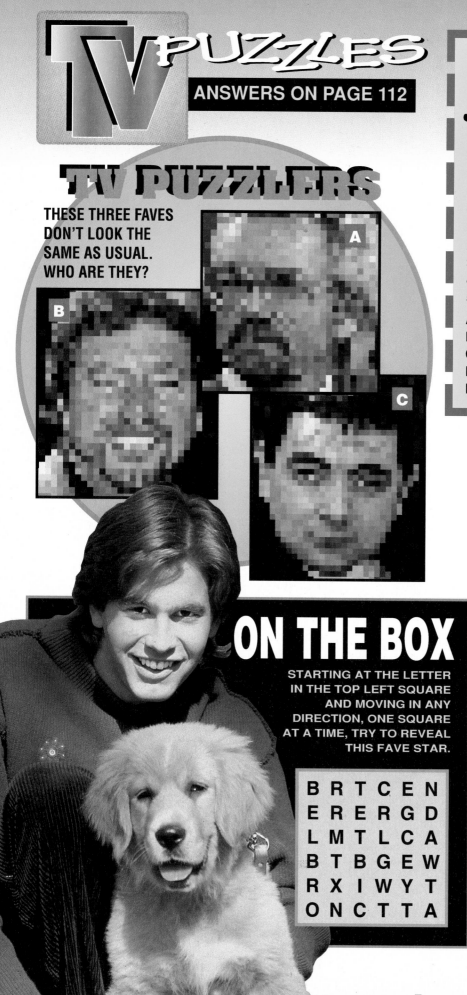

THESE THREE FAVES DON'T LOOK THE SAME AS USUAL. WHO ARE THEY?

A

B

C

ON THE BOX

STARTING AT THE LETTER IN THE TOP LEFT SQUARE AND MOVING IN ANY DIRECTION, ONE SQUARE AT A TIME, TRY TO REVEAL THIS FAVE STAR.

B	R	T	C	E	N
E	R	E	R	G	D
L	M	T	L	C	A
B	T	B	G	E	W
R	X	I	W	Y	T
O	N	C	T	T	A

pro
star

You've thirty seconds to matc the names of th stars with the shows they host

1. CILLA BLACK
2. LES DENNIS
3. NOEL EDMONDS
4. JIM DAVIDSON
5. NICKY CAMPBELL

A. FAMILY FORTUNES
B. THE GENERATION G
C. WHEEL OF FORTUN
D. THE HOUSE PARTY
E. BLIND DATE

SEEIN
STAR

HOW MANY STA CAN YOU COUNT H

TOP STARS

UNSCRAMBLE THE LETTERS TO GIVE THE NAMES OF THESE FAVE GUYS.

A

CLEDAN LONEDYLN

B

IDNA SPREET

C

TINROAM RAZILEZ

Superman

ere are some estions to test ur brainboxes out the BBC's ries, "The ew Adventures Superman". me are easy asy and me are quite cky.

Name the star who plays Superman.

What are the colours of Superman's costume?

What lucky girl is Superman's friend and colleague?

What's her job?

Name the star who plays her.

What did Superman do in real life before becoming a fave star?

What is Superman's name in the series when he's not flying?

Name the substance that Superman's frightened of.

What dreadful effects does it have on him?

10. Give the name of the junior in Superman's office.

11. Name the actor who plays him. (Tricky one.)

12. In which city do the Superhero's adventures take place?

family faves

A. Unscramble the letters to give the names of these two stars.

1. MEGMA IXSSBI
2. LAUP LRBADYE

B. Which soap do they appear in?

C. Fill in the blanks to give the names of the characters they play.

1. CL__E _A_E_
2. N_G_L B_T_S

Superman DEAN CAIN

Lois Lane TERI HATCHER

SUPERMAN

MAY

MONDAY	–	5	12	19	26
TUESDAY	–	6	13	20	27
WEDNESDAY	–	7	14	21	28
THURSDAY	1	8	15	22	29
FRIDAY	2	9	16	23	30
SATURDAY	3	10	17	24	31
SUNDAY	4	11	18	25	–

JUNE

MONDAY	–	2	9	16	23	30
TUESDAY	–	3	10	17	24	–
WEDNESDAY	–	4	11	18	25	–
THURSDAY	–	5	12	19	26	–
FRIDAY	–	6	13	20	27	–
SATURDAY	–	7	14	21	28	–
SUNDAY	1	8	15	22	29	–

JULY

MONDAY	–	7	14	21	28
TUESDAY	1	8	15	22	29
WEDNESDAY	2	9	16	23	30
THURSDAY	3	10	17	24	31
FRIDAY	4	11	18	25	–
SATURDAY	5	12	19	26	–
SUNDAY	6	13	20	27	–

AUGUST

MONDAY	–	4	11	18	25
TUESDAY	–	5	12	19	26
WEDNESDAY	–	6	13	20	27
THURSDAY	–	7	14	21	28
FRIDAY	1	8	15	22	29
SATURDAY	2	9	16	23	30
SUNDAY	3	10	17	24	31

Jimmy Olsen JUSTIN WHALIN

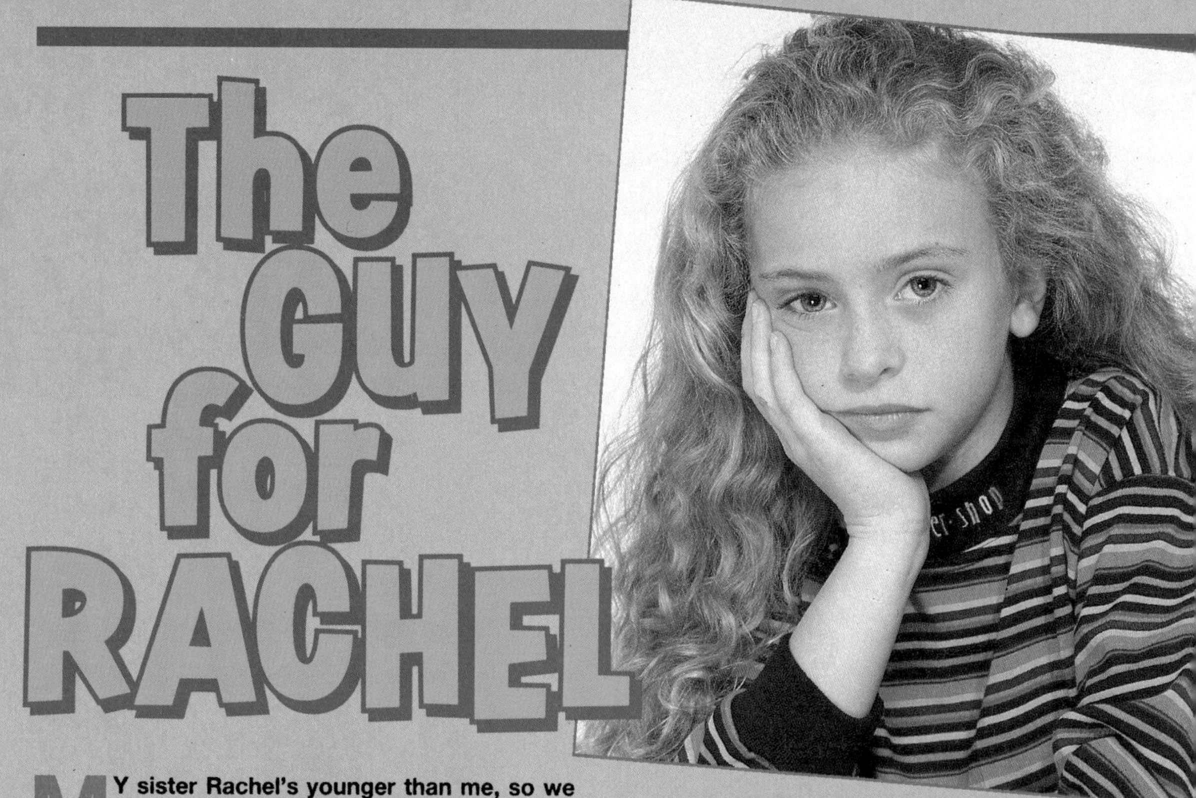

The GUY for RACHEL

MY sister Rachel's younger than me, so we don't see much of each other at school. But, one day she rushed over to me in the playground and pointed across to two boys in the tuck shop queue.

"Do you know them?" she asked.

"Yes," I replied. "Alan and Rob. They're in my year."

"Well, I really fancy Rob. Help me get a date with him," she begged.

I was horrified!

"No way!" I told her. "I'm not getting involved in anything like that."

And I kept on refusing — even when she offered me her latest Blur tape as a bribe.

I was hoping Rachel would forget all about it, but she didn't — and then Miss Knight asked me to dress up as a fortune teller at the school fête . . .

"This is your chance to help me!" Rachel squealed excitedly, when she heard the news. "Everyone's bound to have their fortune told! It'll be a laugh, so, when Rob comes in to your tent, tell him to ask me out. Say it's written in the stars or something!"

I was going to say no again, but then I thought about it. Maybe using my fortune-telling disguise to do a bit of matchmaking wasn't a bad idea.

On the day of the fête I was really busy. All the teachers and pupils wanted their fortunes told, it seemed. Of course, the teachers knew I couldn't really see into the future, and that it was just a laugh to raise money for charity — but a lot of the kids really believed I had special powers.

It was a long while before Alan and Rob turned up, but at last they did. They walked into the tent together and sat down in front of me. After they'd crossed my palm with silver (fifty pence actually), I looked into my crystal ball and started to talk in my best Mystic Meg voice.

"There's this girl in the year below you," began. "Her name's Rachel."

By the time I got home from the fête, Racl was already back.

"Well? Did he ask you out?" I asked eagerly. told him to!"

"You told the WRONG guy!" Rachel repli angrily. "You told ALAN — and he came and ask me out. But it was ROB I fancied!"

I groaned.

"Oh, no! I'm really sorry, Rachel. I always g those two mixed up. It must be cos they both ha the same hair colour."

"Huh! They're not at all alike," Rachel snappe "Rob's much nicer — and I'm definitely NOT goi out with Alan!

"You must!" I insisted. "I told him you rea liked him. If you turn him down now, he'll know r fortune-telling act was a scam. I'll lose my stre cred."

In the end I persuaded Rachel she had to go. she went — but she wasn't pleased. It was different story when she came back, though.

"Alan's a bit of all right," she enthused. "He much nicer than Rob. In fact, I don't know wha ever saw in Rob."

"So you're seeing Alan again?" I asked.

"Oh, yes. We're going out at the weekend and it's all thanks to you!" Rachel replied happi "I'm really glad you mixed up Rob and Alan now!"

I smiled sweetly and said nothing. You se there HADN'T been a mix-up! I know which boy Alan and which is Rob. I MEANT to tell Alan to a Rachel out. It WASN'T a mistake at all. I'd fanci Rob for yonks. Being a fortune teller at the fê gave me just the chance I needed to suggest th he went out with ME!

make 'n' do

ke yourself a cool mirror with a funky frame to hang in your room.

It's dead simple and looks great.

OU'LL NEED:

- large plain paper plate
- nall amounts of paint
- nulsion matchpots are
- eal)
- oonge
- ue
- aft Varnish
- irror (We used an old
- ake-up mirror with a broken
- me. Look out for these at
- r boot or garage sales and
- t an Old to remove the
- me for you. Discount
- ores are other good places
- look.)

We used a flower pattern on our mirror, but you could try hearts, fish, triangles, stars and moons — or just about anything you like.

1. Dip a torn-off piece of sponge into the paint. Dab off any excess on a piece of scrap paper. Gently start to dab the paint on to the paper plate.

2. Cover the whole plate with paint.

3. Cut a small circle and a petal shape from the sponge. Use them to sponge on a flower pattern. Work your way round the plate — it doesn't matter if some of the petals overlap.

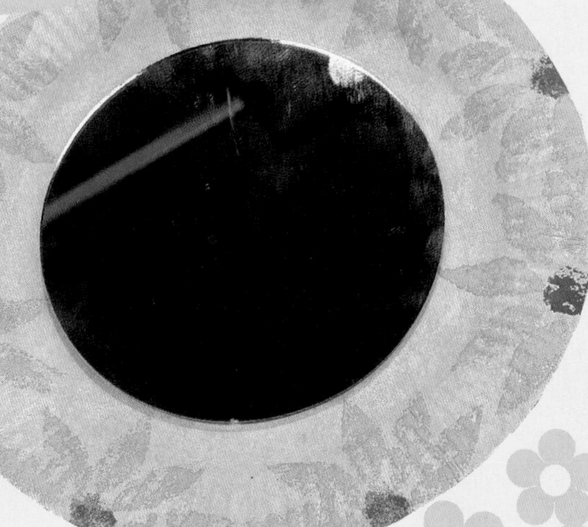

4. When you have a pattern all ound the plate, let it dry properly. To make e mirror frame harder, cover with a couple of coats of craft varnish. Let that dry. Now you can stick on your mirror. Use a strong craft glue like UHU. Stick a loop of ribbon to the back for hanging the mirror. When it's dry, hang it up. Easy, eh?

Furry Friends

Aww! Check out this bunch of fluffy, cuddly cuties — they're gorgeo
And all these star pets belong to you lot. Is yours there?

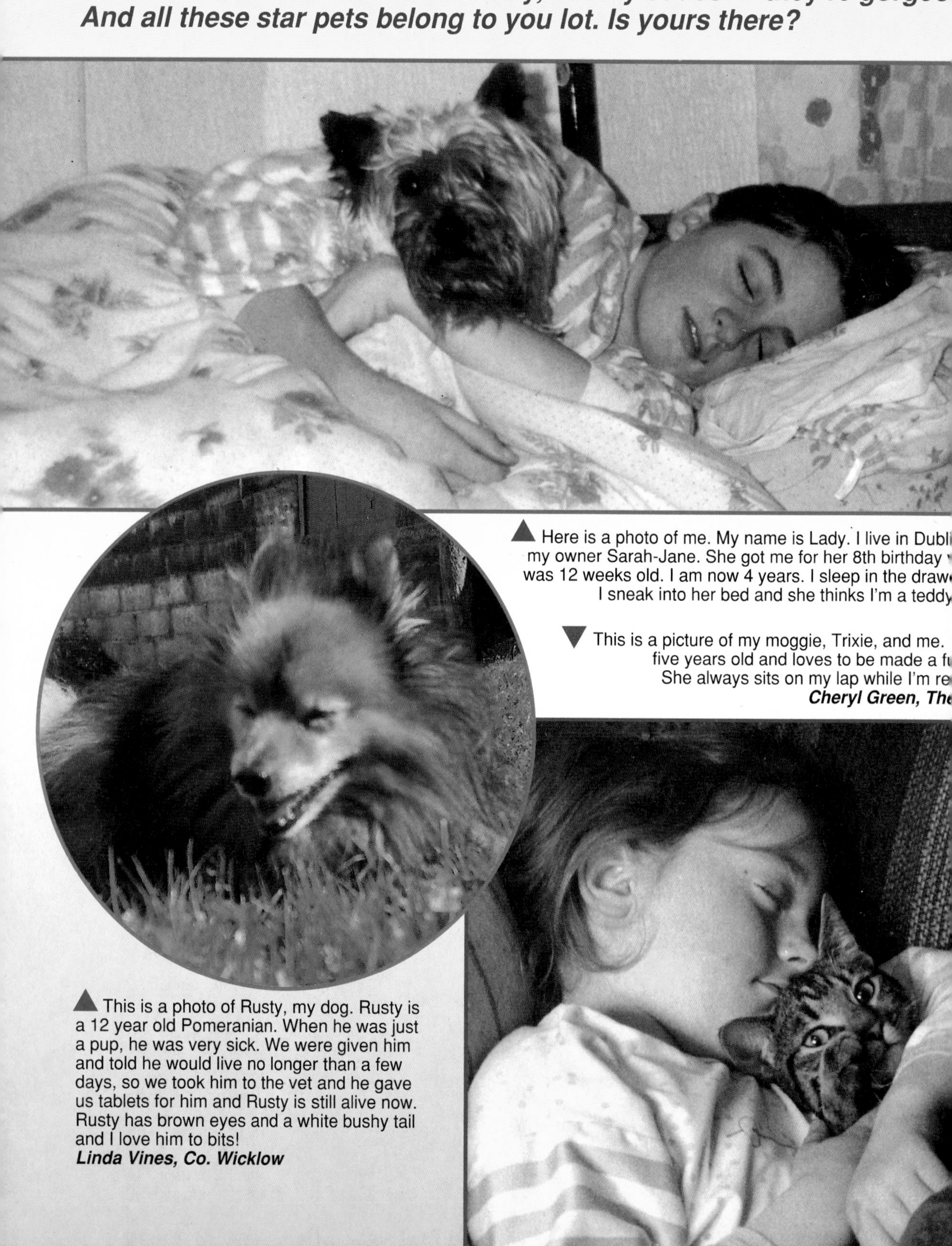

▲ Here is a photo of me. My name is Lady. I live in Dubl
my owner Sarah-Jane. She got me for her 8th birthday
was 12 weeks old. I am now 4 years. I sleep in the draw
I sneak into her bed and she thinks I'm a teddy

▼ This is a picture of my moggie, Trixie, and me.
five years old and loves to be made a f
She always sits on my lap while I'm re
Cheryl Green, Th

▲ This is a photo of Rusty, my dog. Rusty is a 12 year old Pomeranian. When he was just a pup, he was very sick. We were given him and told he would live no longer than a few days, so we took him to the vet and he gave us tablets for him and Rusty is still alive now. Rusty has brown eyes and a white bushy tail and I love him to bits!
Linda Vines, Co. Wicklow

This is my dog Cindy. I really love her. She is a West
ıland White Terrier and she is really, really cute.
da Keane, Enniscorthy

This is a picture of my cat, Thomas. He came to our
ily as a stray. We tried hard to get rid of him, but he
sed to go. In the end we gave in and kept him.
mas is so soft and cuddly. I would love to see his
to printed and so would he!
re McClelland, Ballinamallard

This is a photo of my Rough Collie, Gemma. I've written this poem about her.

've got a dog called Gemma,
She really is a pain,
When the house is comfy,
She goes out in the rain,
She shakes out all the water,
All over every guest,
She really is a torture,
She really is a pest,
But we do love her!

Nicola Dyke, Swansea

▲ This is my moggie, Tabatha. She always sleeps with her white blanket. Sometimes, when I'm reading, she will come over and try to see what I'm doing. Please print her photo.
Anna Wilkinson, Edinburgh

▲ Hi! I'm Amy. I don't have a cat because my mum's allergic to them. This is George, my gran's cat, in my pushchair! He has a sister called Emma. They're used to children and they're both softies!
Amy Child, Leeds

Pig Out!

Check out these recipes. They're all great for midnight feasts, sleep-ove[r] parties, or makin[g] on dull days. They're all sent in by you lot. They [a]... win £5. They're all easy and they're all YUMMY!

Remember — always ask an adult bef[ore] using any kitchen equipment.

Slug Sweets

They're disgustingly delicious!

Ingredients

1 box of stoned dates
90g of icing sugar
2 tablespoons of cocoa powder
50g soft butter

Method

1. Mix the sugar, cocoa and butter together to form a smooth creamy paste.
2. Cover the dates all over in the paste. Mould the dates into a slug-like shape.
3. Put into the fridge to chill.
4. EAT!

Morwenna Rowlands, Lydbrook

Chocolate Mud Pies

Ingredients

225g hard margarine
225g plain flour
100g sugar
50g cornflakes
1 heaped tablespoon cocoa

Method

1. Cream margarine and sugar until soft and fluffy.
2. Sieve cocoa and flour together. Add to the creamy mixture.
3. Crush cornflakes together till crumbly and add to the mixture.
4. Place in small heaps on a greased baking tray using a fork.
5. Bake in moderate oven, 150°C (300°F, Gas Mark 2) until firm. This takes approximately 20-30 minutes. Yum! Yum!

Mary Darby, Thetford

Choccy & Raisin Sl[ice]

Ingredients

60g butter
14 crushed digestive biscuits
120g chocolate
125g raisins
Small tin of condense[d] milk

Method

1. Melt butter and chocolate in a pan over l[ow] heat.
2. Remove from heat a[nd] stir in raisins and condensed milk.
3. Add mixture to crush[ed] digestives and stir well.
4. Press mix down firml[y] into a Swiss roll tray.
5. Leave to set (do not put in the fridge).
6. Cut into slices and scoff!

Rose Yu, Leeds

Banana Chocolate Chip Cookies

Ingredients

100g plain flour
1/2 tsp baking powder
1/4 tsp salt
175g light brown sugar
75g white sugar
225g butter or margarine
1 egg
100g Kellogg's Banana Bubbles
175g chocolate chips

Method

1. Combine flour, salt and baking powder.
2. Mix the two types of sugar in a large bowl, add the butter or margarine and mix well together.
3. Add the egg and mix well.
4. Add remaining ingredients and blend together.
5. Drop rounded tablespoons of mixture o[n]to a greased baking tray 5 cm apart.
6. Bake at 150°C (300°F or Gas Mark 2) for 20-25 minutes.
7. Allow to cool slightly before removing from tra[y]. Makes 50 cookies!

Kerry Thomas, Pickerin[g]

Coconut Hedgehogs

Ingredients
- ?0 g flour
- ?nch of salt
- ?easpoon baking ?owder
- ?g margarine
- ?g caster sugar
- ?0g coconut
- ?egg
- ?4 tablespoons milk

?ecoration:
- ?4 tbsp warmed jam
- ?5 tbsp coconut
- ?aisins or choc chips

?ethod
?. Sieve flour, salt and ?aking powder into a ?owl.
?. Rub in margarine until ?ixture resembles breadcrumbs. Stir in sugar and coconut and mix.
3. Beat egg. Add a little milk and pour this into centre of mixture, adding enough milk to make a stiff dough.
4. Using a spoon and fork, put 12 piles of mixture on a greased baking tray.
5. Bake in a fairly hot oven, 215°C/425°F/Gas Mark 6 for 20 minutes.
6. Put jam and coconut on 2 plates. Dip cooled buns into warm jam, then into coconut. Stick on raisins or choc chips for eyes.

Marion Courtney, Co. Kenny

Sponge Fairy Cakes

from Katie Sherry, Glasgow

Ingredients
- 100g self raising flour
- 100g sugar
- 100g butter/margarine
- 2 eggs

Method
Pre-heat the oven to 200°C (or Gas Mark 6/400°F).
1. Sift the flour into a large bowl and add the sugar, butter/margarine and the 2 eggs.
2. Beat well until it becomes a thick smooth mixture.
3. Get a bun tray and put paper cases into each place.
4. Put equal amounts of the mixture into each case and bake for 12-15 minutes.

The cakes should be golden and springy when they're ready. When they're cool sprinkle with icing sugar or turn them into

Kangaroo Eyes

Clare McDonnell from Co. Tipperary tells you how.

You need
12 fairy cakes
2-3 kiwi fruits, sliced and peeled
1 packet of orange flavour Quick-gel

1. Make the Quick-gel as instructed on packet.
2. When Quick-gel has cooled, place a slice of kiwi fruit on each cake.
3. Coat the kiwi fruit in Quick-gel.
4. Leave the Quick-gel to set and then tuck in!

Yummy Toffee Crispy Bars

Ingredients
- 100g butter
- 100g marshmallows
- 100g toffees or caramels
- 100g Rice Krispies

Method
1. Melt the butter, marshmallows and toffees together in a saucepan and boil for about 1-2 minutes.
2. Take the pan off the heat and fold in the Rice Krispies.
3. Spread into a greased baking tray, leave to set for about 10-15 minutes and cut into squares. Mmm!

Becky Hill, Stow-on-the-Wold

?idnight Mints

?gredients
- ?heaped ?blespoons of icing ?gar
- ?eaped ?blespoons of ?coa
- ?ablespoons of ?k
- ?ablespoon of ?tter or ?rgarine
- ? drops of ?ppermint ?ence
- ?owl of melted ?colate or ?oa powder

Method
1. Put the icing sugar, cocoa, milk, butter or marg and peppermint essence into a mixing bowl and mix to a thick paste with a wooden spoon.
2. With your fingers break off lumps of the mixture about the size of a walnut and shape them into small balls.
3. When the mixture is dry roll each ball in melted chocolate or cocoa powder.
4. Now leave the Midnight Mints in the fridge for an hour to chill before eating.

Aisling Carey, Mullingar

Almond And Coconut Munchies

?gredients
- ?g Rice Krispies
- ?g ground almonds
- ?g desiccated coconut
- ?0g milk chocolate
- ?ablespoons golden syrup
- ?g margarine
- ?ew flaked almonds to decorate

?ethod
?. Put the margarine, chocolate and golden syrup into a bowl and melt in a microwave at Mark 1 or in a saucepan over low heat.
2. Then add the ground almonds, Rice Krispies and coconut to the mixture and mix quickly.
3. Put it into a shallow greased dish and place the flaked almonds on top.
4. Leave to set then cut into squares.
5. Munch!

Fiona Riordan, Glanmire

FIGURE IT OUT! ge

Amaze peeps by revealing some of their innermost secrets.

...But first you must find out your special lucky number between one and nine. Once you know try to follow it as much as possible for loadsa lu

FIRST

NOW HERE'S HOW TO FIGURE OUT ANYONE'S SPECIAL LUCKY NUMBER.

Each letter of the alphabet has a number, as follows:

A	-	1
B	-	2
C	-	3
D	-	4
E	-	5
F	-	8
G	-	3
H	-	5
I	-	1
J	-	1
K	-	2
L	-	3
M	-	4
N	-	5
O	-	7
P	-	8
Q	-	1
R	-	2
S	-	3
T	-	4
U	-	6
V	-	6
W	-	6
X	-	5
Y	-	1
Z	-	7

SECOND

You're wanting to find a lucky number from 1 - 9, so calculate as follows:
To find a lucky number, use someone's Christian name AND surname. For example, if your name's JANE SMITH, you'd work out your number like this using the numbers given in the FIRST panel.

J	-	1
A	-	1
N	-	5
E	-	5
Total	=	12

S	-	3
M	-	4
I	-	1
T	-	4
H	-	5
Total	=	17

Then add the above totals:
(12) 1 + 2 = **3** (17) 1 + 7 = **8**

Now add the totals (3 and 8):
3 + 8 = 11

Now add the total (11):
1 + 1 = 2

JANE'S lucky number is TWO.

Work out each peep's name separately, as shown, adding the totals together as in the example.

Keep adding until you end up with a number UNDER ten. (If someone is known by a nickname, work out the number by using the name that peep is most commonly called.)

e.g. If someone's name is Katherine but she's always called Kate, use Kate to work out her number. So now you know how it works, get those lucky numbers figured out!

1. One is your lucky number? You think about yourself a lot and you're a little vain. Try walking past that mirror sometimes and giving other peeps a second thought. On the positive side, you're generous, look on the bright side of things and are good at making decisions.

The numbers you get along best with are 2, 4 and especially 7. If a guy from one of these groups comes along, you'll get on grea

2. Wakey, Wakey! If 2 is your lucky number, you're very much a dreamer. You can spend hours just thinking. You're gentle natured, artistic and romantic. However, you love really bright colours and way out gear. They make you feel wildly different.

You may have probs being friends with guys or girls who have 2 as their lucky number, but you'll be able to have an easy-going and lasting relationships with peeps with numbers 1 and 7.

3. So three's your lucky number? Well, pat yourself on the back. You're a pretty lucky person! If you want something, you usually get it and you're charming and talented. However, you have a tendency to be bossy and you like being the centre of attraction.

Your ideal friend would be someone with the numbers 6 or 9.

ow more about yourself using numbers.

● Your lucky
nber's 4. That
ans you've got it
going for you.
're lively, popular
bright and will
ays attract friends.
rebel in you
kes you in great
nand when people
t cheering up.
've loadsa friends
despite this,
're often lonely
find it difficult to
t people.

You'll really
t off with peeps
have 1 as their
ky number.

5● If your lucky number's 5, you just lurve being the centre of attention. Because you want people to like you, you're nice to everyone, tolerant and generous to a fault. This means you get put upon at times. That's all to the good.

You're one of the few peeps who could make a success of a relationship with anyone from any number group.

6● Your lucky number's six? This means you love travel, new places and new peeps. You can be a bit shallow with your relationships though and people are often thrown and don't know where they stand with you.

Those you're most likely to get on the best with, have the lucky numbers 3 or 6.

7● If you're a number seven, you're outrageous, independent and a wild extrovert. You just lurve creating a stir wherever you go and are often very imaginative with what you wear. This means you can be a bit of a show-off.

You'll infuriate and fascinate anyone around you. This is just what you like!

The ideal guy for you would be a 2. He's the only number likely to tame you.

● If your lucky number is eight, you
e showing off entertaining. When
're in a good mood, you like everyone
they all like you. The trouble is that,
en you're down in the dumps, you've
time for anyone
want to lie
ut feeling sorry
yourself. It's
gh on anyone
expects you to
full of life at that
e!

You'll get on
t with peeps who
a 4 or 8.

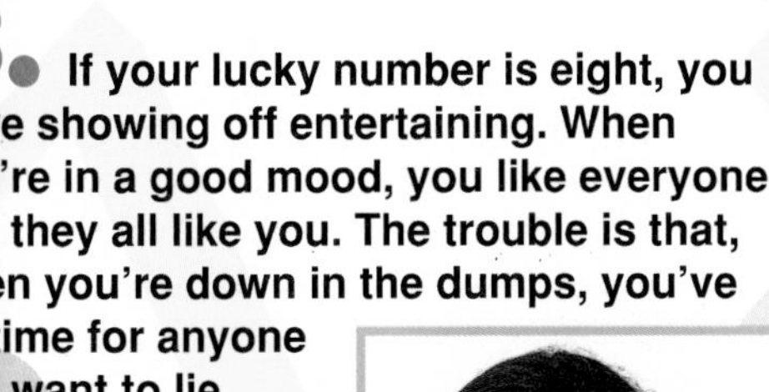

9● So you're a number nine! Chances are you'll spend a lot of your time studying. You're never happier than when you're up to your elbows in text books. Exceptionally neat and tidy, you can be very tolerant of other peeps who aren't the same way inclined as you.

A 3 or a 6 is your ideal partner. They can put up with you and, if you can learn to relax, you could have a lot of fun in their company.

ntinued from page 53

copy kat

You okay, Rachel? You nearly fell!
I can *SEE* it is! I've struggled up here for *NOTHING! AND* I nearly hurt myself!
It's a squirrel!

A few minutes later —
Rachel Mason, you're a foolish girl.
Huh! They've all had a good laugh at my expense.

t, later, when Rachel told Harriet —
. . . then I discovered it was only a squirrel. Ha! Ha!
I won't say it was embarrassing, that I nearly fell, and I was trying to be like a character in my mag.
What an interesting story, Rachel!

Next day —
Was your mum annoyed about your torn skirt then, Rachel?
A bit — well, *A LOT!*
It was funny, but you were great. We might be looking at a future head girl here!

hen —
What's Kat up to this week? Oh! She's in a rollathon, just like I was! But *SHE* manages to rescue someone from danger on the way round!

She's first across the line and massive crowds cheer her. So it wasn't really like me! Yet I wouldn't have been in the rollathon at all if I hadn't been trying to be more like Kat! Oh, I'm all mixed up!

Come on, Rachel, get your room tidied. Aunt Liz is coming! Throw out all these old magazines.
No, not those, Mum!
The Kat stories are in those! Oh, I *HATE* it when Aunt Liz visits! She's so full of herself.

Soon —
And what have *YOU* been doing late Rachel. *I'VE* been so busy!
Typical! Aunt Liz asks me about myself then talks about *HERSELF!*

A little later —
Oh! I promised Harriet next door my chocolate cake recipe. Will you take it round now, Rachel?
I'll be glad to get away from Aunt Liz. I'd rather see Harriet!

And so —
What's your school like for clubs and societies, Rachel? Any good ones?
Um . . . yes, there are loads, Harriet.

You must tell me all about them . . . Oh, excuse me, there's the phone.
I'll just go, Harriet, I'll speak to you later.
Kat would be in loads of school clubs. Maybe I should look into joining a few.

So, next day —
SCHOOL CLUBS
Disco dance club? Brilliant! That's after school today. I'll join. And the environmental group meet this lunch-time. I'll go along!

lunch-time —
GREEN
RLD
We're going to do something about the environment today. We're going to pick up litter.
I've joined a club to pick up litter? Never mind! It's the disco dance class after school. That'll be good!

So, later —
This is more like it. Mega music!

t —
I'm sorry I've stopped your music, but I've got to have the electricity switched off. We have a problem with the circuit.
That's TWO of my club sessions gone wrong!

Later that evening at Harriet's —
. . . and then I was late home because I missed the bus. What a day!
How busy and interesting you are, Rachel!
I'm not interesting at all! My day sounded good to Harriet because of the way I told it. I'm a fake! I tried to be like Kat and failed!

hen, one morning —
ve got this week's g. Now to see what Kat's up to.
Hey, guess what, Janie! This week Kat joins an environmental group, just like I did.
Oh, Rachel, you're not still taking these stories seriously, are you? Come on! We'll be late for school.

I wonder what Janie would say if she knew I've been trying to be like Kat? I'd like to have more confidence. Anyway, I'm dying to read the story and see what happens to her.

A few minutes later —
Ooh, Kat discovers something toxic being dumped in a river and reports it. Trust Kat! She joined an environmental group, just like I did, but things *HAPPEN* to her!

Suddenly —
And what *HAVE* we here? Not exac reference work I planned for you, Rac can catch up at lunch-time in deten Meanwhile *I'LL* keep this!

After school —
Coming then, Rachel? We're going round the shops in town.
Sure I'm coming, Janie! I've had enough of being on my own today.

Soon —
That top's gorgeous. It would suit you, Rachel. It's your fave colour.
Mm, I might buy it at the weekend.
I'm feeling better now. I've decided to give up wondering what Kat would do all the time, and just be myself.

Look at that toddler!
Oh, no!
He must have wandered away from his mum — and that lorry's reversing!

I have to get him out of the way — *FAST*!

Oh, thank you. Thank you so much. Oh, I can't thank you enough. My baby!
Rachel, you were just like your heroine!
You were brilliant, Rachel! So quick!
But I wasn't trying to be like Kat, for once. I just acted instinctively, as myself. I don't think I need Kat any more!

That evening —
I'll tell Harriet what happened in town. She likes hearing all my news!

w minutes later —
What are you doing with all these teenage magazines, Harriet?
I'm a writer, Rachel, and my stories are in these magazines. I keep them for reference.

Yes, I write stories for girls. And I have to tell you, Rachel — you've helped me.
I've HELPED you? HOW?

Well, I created a character called Kat. I used things you told me to get ideas for the stories. Of course, I used to exaggerate and add all sorts of stuff.

So, while I've been trying to be like Kat, Kat was really like ME! That feels strange! But I don't need to try to be like anybody else, anyway. I'm okay, just as I am!
THE END

CHRISTMAS PUZZLES

snow flakes

HOW MANY SNOWFLAKES CAN YOU SEE?

star gifts

Answer each group o
correctly and the sha
squares, reading dow
will spell out what ea
wants for Christmas.
forget to name the st
(Easy peasy!)

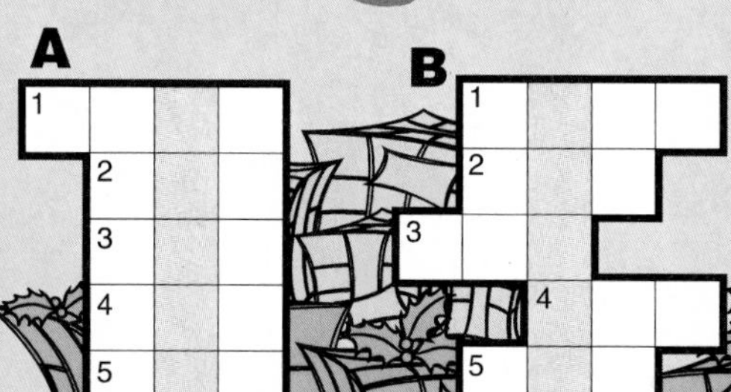

A....................

B....................

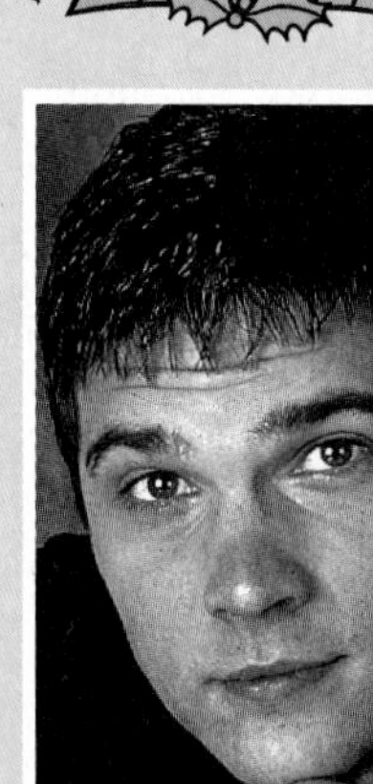

C..................

A

1. One more than four
2. Small, sharp metal object
3. Opposite of subtract
4. Large expanse of salty water
5. Man's best friend

B

1. Not shut
2. You write with it
3. Not near
4. Have this at the fair
5. Sharp pull
6. Mischievous little creature
7. Caused by sadness

C

1. Not wild
2. Opposite light
3. Precious found in sh
4. Not full

Missing goodies

There are letters missing fro the alphabet. Find out wh they are then re-arrange them to find something you might eat at Christm

A B C D F G H I J L M N O P Q S V W X Z

pot santa

These three stars are playing Father Christmas. Can you spot who's under the disguises?

A

B

C

sleigh bells

These are all names of Father Christmas's reindeers - except one. Which is the odd one out?

RUDOLPH	LEAPER	DASHER
BLITZEN	DANCER	PRANCER
	DONNER	

CHRISSIE WORDS

ADD ONE OF THESE LETTERS TO THE CORRECT GROUP OF SCRAMBLED LETTERS SO THAT, WHEN THE LETTERS ARE UNSCRAMBLED, EACH GROUP MAKES A WORD CONNECTED WITH CHRISTMAS.

N R O F L

A. ETE_

....

TIELR_

....

EIRREED_

....

WNS_

....

LOYH_

....

Oh, No It's Not!

The names of FIVE pantomimes have got jumbled up. Can you sort things out?

MOTHER BABES

CINDERELLA AND THE BEANSTALK

ALADDIN IN THE WOOD

JACK GOOSE

ANSWERS ON PAGE 112

crimbly deccies

WHICH TWO CHRISTMAS BAUBLES ARE IDENTICAL?

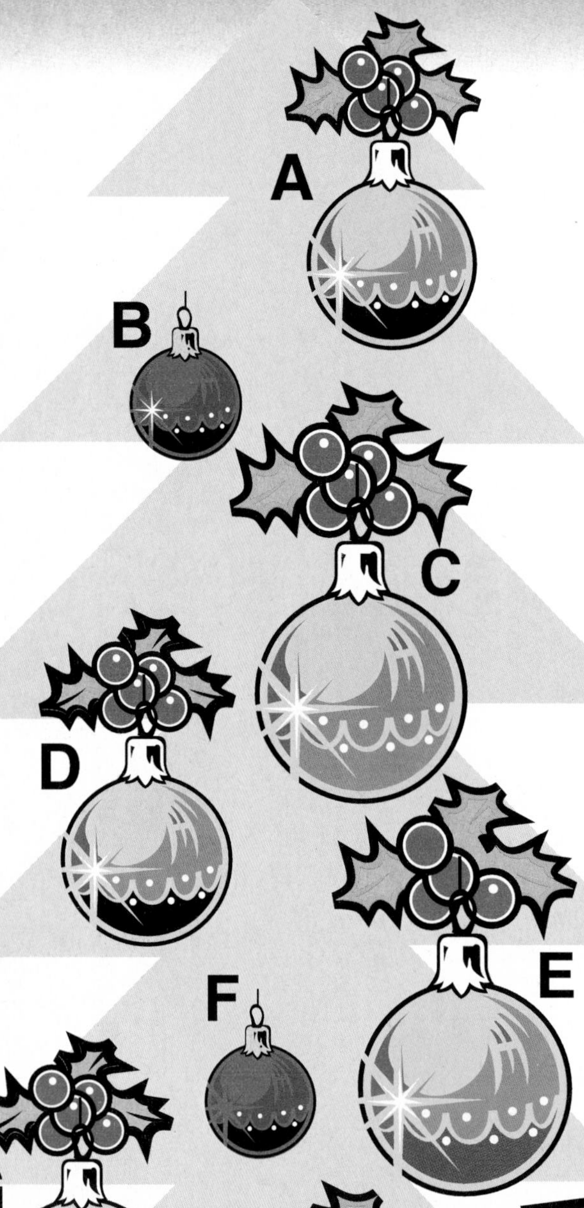

ANSWERS ON PAGE 112

CHRISTMA

FESTIVE NAM

Complete the puzzle by filling in your answers, reading downwards, on the panels. Each letter of Santa's name star off an answer.

1. Lettuce and veg, eaten raw.
2. A crunchy fruit.
3. Dark part of a day.
4. Piece of furniture for eating at
5. Venomous snake.

chrissie cross out

Cross out the letters which appear four times, or more to leave the name of something you'd love to at Christmas

A	T	J	C	Y	M
W	M	M	R	M	B
Y	I	A	B	J	W
W	F	Y	B	C	A
C	M	L	J	M	W
J	A	B	Y	E	C

cracking crimbo

Write your answers to the clues in the spaces provided. They all have something to do with Christmas. If your answers are correct, you'll find them in the grid. Letters can be used more than once and the Christmas words read upwards, downwards, backwards, forwards or diagonally.

1. Very short name for Father Christmas..........................
2. A song sung at Christmas..........................
3. It goes bang and holds a gift..........................
4. Prickly evergreen with red berries..........................
5. Red breasted little bird..........................
6. Electricity makes them shine..........................
7. Santa's four-legged, red-nosed helper..........................
8. Santa travels on this..........................
9. It comes wrapped in paper..........................
10. You're kissed under this!..........................
11. Bells do this on Christmas morning..........................
12. Wax shape that burns brightly..........................
13. It shines in the night..........................
14. Traditional Christmas bird..........................
15. It is decorated at the festive season..........................
16. We sign it and post it..........................
17. Kind of animal that pulls Santa along..........................

E	E	R	T	H	G	N	I	R	M
R	U	D	O	L	P	H	A	C	I
G	E	L	L	A	T	N	A	S	S
S	L	E	I	G	H	R	T	C	T
Y	D	R	G	E	O	T	R	C	L
E	N	A	H	L	N	A	R	A	E
K	A	T	T	E	C	I	W	R	T
R	C	S	S	K	B	G	B	D	O
U	P	R	E	S	E	N	T	O	E
T	L	R	E	E	D	N	I	E	R

christmas guests

These guys are looking forward to Christmas. Name them and unscramble the letters to find out what pressie they've brought. Easy for bright bods like you!

IT was the day before Christmas Eve and Lisa Grant was thinking about Christmas presents —

Game Boy
Date with Jamie

That's my Christmas list. That's what I'd really like more than anything, but there's no chance of either. Game Boys are too expensive and I think Jamie fancies Cara.

Christmas Wish

I saw Jamie talking to Cara at school on the last day. I bet he was asking if he could take her to the Christmas Eve disco. I don't know if I'll bother to go.

Later that day, Gran arrived.
I've got . . . um . . . some things in my bag. You know . . .
Gran means she's brought our presents and she doesn't want me to know. She's done this since I was little.

Have you written your letter to Santa Claus, Lisa? I hope you've been a good girl all year. Santa Claus knows if you haven't.
Yes, I know, Gran.
She thinks I still believe in Santa Claus. It's dead embarrassing when she talks to me as if I'm a little kid.
Lisa, will you go to the shops for me, love? I've forgotten the cornflour.
That's a good idea. Then I can . . . er . . . sort out my shopping bag.
few minutes later —
Gran thinks she's fooling me. On Christmas morning there'll be a lovely present from her, but she'll say she had to send it through Santa Claus.
Then —
That old man's fallen. He probably slipped on a patch of ice.
Are you okay?
Here, take my jacket. I'm going to run back home for help. Won't be a minute.
Thank you, my dear.
Soon —
He says his name's Mr Jones, Mum.
Come on then, Mr Jones, we'll get you to the hospital.

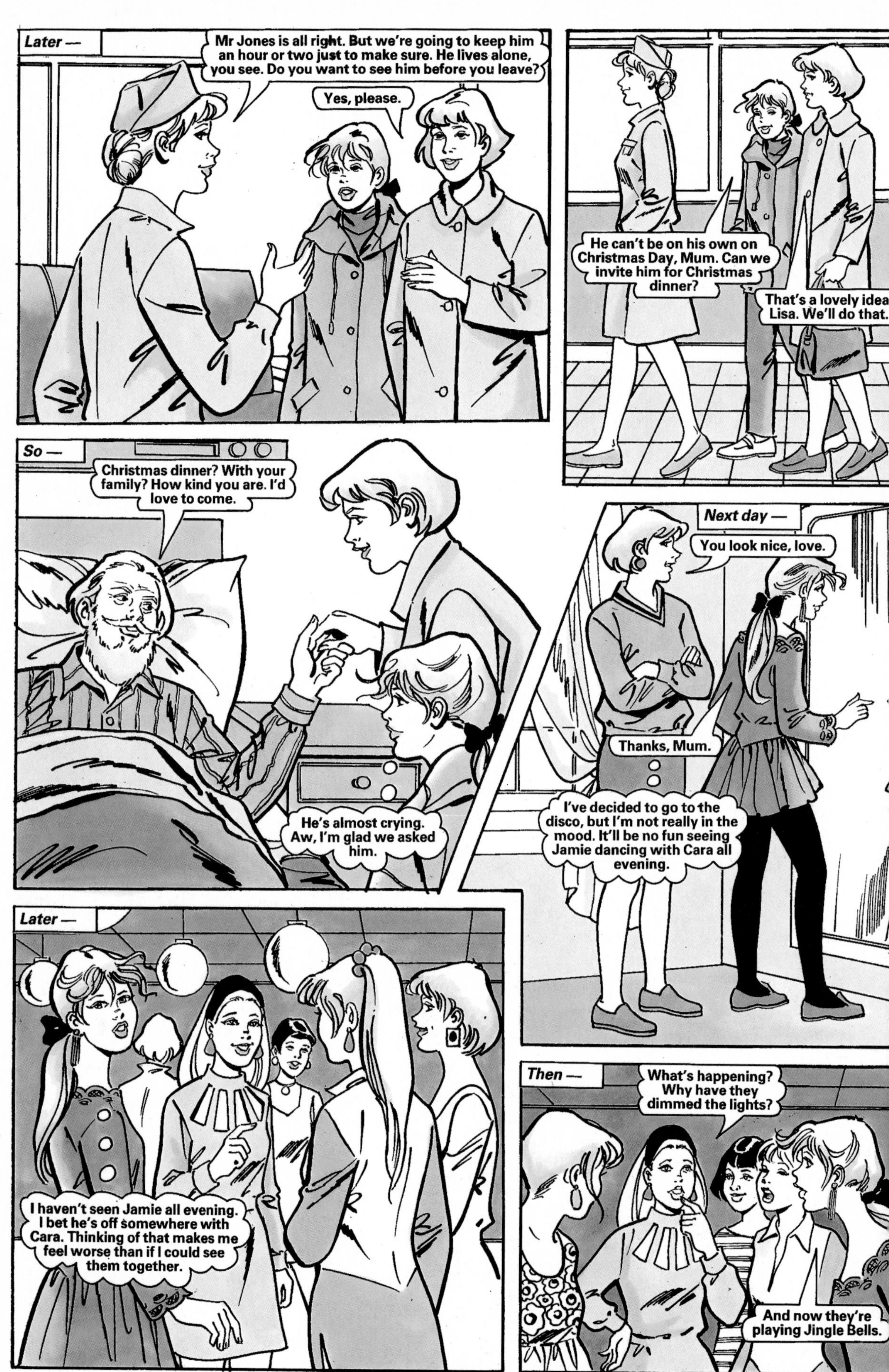
Later —
Mr Jones is all right. But we're going to keep him an hour or two just to make sure. He lives alone, you see. Do you want to see him before you leave?
Yes, please.
He can't be on his own on Christmas Day, Mum. Can we invite him for Christmas dinner?
That's a lovely idea Lisa. We'll do that.
So —
Christmas dinner? With your family? How kind you are. I'd love to come.
He's almost crying. Aw, I'm glad we asked him.
Next day —
You look nice, love.
Thanks, Mum.
I've decided to go to the disco, but I'm not really in the mood. It'll be no fun seeing Jamie dancing with Cara all evening.
Later —
I haven't seen Jamie all evening. I bet he's off somewhere with Cara. Thinking of that makes me feel worse than if I could see them together.
Then —
What's happening? Why have they dimmed the lights?
And now they're playing Jingle Bells.

Oh, it's Santa Claus. I don't believe this.
That's really uncool! They must think we're junior school kids.
But look at Mr Turner. He organised this disco and he doesn't seem to know what's going on, either.

wever —
Santa has a little gift for everyone.
anta is for kids. But I suppose we'd better not say anything. It is Christmas, after all, and we don't want to spoil the disco.

Sorry, Lisa, I don't seem to have yours. I probably dropped it in the classroom where I got changed. Maybe you can go and get it yourself?
Er . . . yes, thank you.
How does he know my name?

a few minutes later —
My pressie is bigger than everyone else's. I wonder . . . oh, there's Jamie.

Hi.
Hi, Lisa, how's the disco going? I've been stuck helping in the coffee bar all evening.
With Cara, I suppose.

Is Cara helping, too?
No, she's not, thank goodness. It's not a nice thing to say, but I can't stand her.

Actually, Lisa . . . er . . . I was coming to look for you. I thought we could dance a bit and . . . well . . . can I take you home afterwards?
I'd like that, Jamie.
Brilliant. He likes ME! I can hardly believe it.

Later —
Will you go out with me on Boxing Day, Lisa?
Love to, Jamie.
It's not even Christmas Day yet, but this is the best Christmas ever.

Next morning —
Here's Mr Jones. He's late. I hope he likes the present we bought for him.
He was having a long lie-ir this morning. Something about a busy night, though can't think what he would b busy doing.

Merry Christmas, Mr Jones.
Thank you. This is really kind of you all.

Later —
This is the present I got last night at the disco. I was so thrilled about being with Jamie that I forgot all about it.

VOW! It's a Game Boy.
Who did you say this was from, Lisa?

It's from Santa, Gran.

I think Gran's right. Maybe there is a Santa after all. And I have a sneaky feeling I know who he is.

THE END

PUZZLE ANSWERS

PAGES 34 to 37

HUNKY GUYS:
A. David Duchovny;
B. Damon Albarn;
C. Ant McPartlin;
D. Christian Slater.
TV HUNK:
1. black; 2. eggs; 3. night; 4. June; 5. idle; 6. Mars; 7. cat; 8. nap; 9. apple; 10. ice; 11. round. (BENJI McNAIR).
STAR INITIALS:
1. Dean Cain;
2. Mark Owen;
3. Martino Lazzeri;
4. David Duchovny. (Cold).
STAR QUIZ:
1. Sean Maguire;
2. Grange Hill;
3. Tegs;
4. EastEnders;
5. Aiden Brosnan;
6. Pop star.
NAME THE GUYS:
A. Michael French;
B. Jaason Simmons;
C. Keanu Reeves.
POP PERSON:
1. Brian Harvey;
2. East 17.
WHO IS IT?:
A. David Chokachi;
B. Baywatch.
PAIRS:
Daniel Amalm; Damon Albarn; David Ginola; Declan Donnelly; David Hasselhof.
BITS 'N' PIECES:
John Alford.
He appears 7 times.
CROSSOUT :
A. Oasis; B. Boyzone.

PAGES 82 to 85

MUDDLED FUN:
1. Dawn French;
2. Lenny Henry;
3. Bob Monkhouse.
GLADIATORS:
1. Wolf;
2. a) Trojan,
 b) Action Man,
 c) Team X-treme,
 d) Mark Griffin;
3. Lightning.
SOAP TIME:
1. a) Angela Griffin,
 b) Coronation Street,
 c) Fiona Middleton;
2. Nic Testoni,
 Home and Away;
3. a) Sam Kratz,
 b) Richard Grieve;
4. a) Patsy Palmer,
 Bianca Jackson,
 b) Dean Gaffney.
TELLY TEST:
1. Fairhead;
2. Top of the Pops;
3. Mark Little and Zoe Ball;
4. Neighbours,
 Joe Mangle;
5. Fully Booked.
STARS IN THEIR EYES:
A. Cilla Black;
B. Dale Winton;
C. Barbara Windsor.
TV PUZZLERS:
A. Noel Edmonds;
B. Jeremy Beadle;
C. Rowan Atkinson.
ON THE BOX:
Brett Blewitt.
PROG STARS:
1 - E; 2 - A;
3 - D; 4 - B;
5 - A.
SEEING STARS:
There are 65 stars.
TOP STARS:
A. Declan Donnelly;
B. Andi Peters;
C. Martino Lazzeri.
SUPERMAN:
1. Dean Cain;
2. Red, blue and yellow;
3. Lois Lane;
4. Reporter;
5. Teri Hatcher;
6. American Football player;
7. Clark Kent;
8. Kryptonite;
9. It weakens him and can kill him;
10. Jimmy Olsen;
11. JustinWhalin;
12. Metropolis.
FAMILY FAVES:
A. 1) Gemma Bissix,
 2) Paul Bradley;
B. EastEnders;
C. 1) Clare Bates,
 2) Nigel Bates.

PAGES 102 to 105

SNOWFLAKES:
There are 40 snowflakes.
STAR GIFTS:
A) 1. five; 2. pin; 3. add; 4. sea; 5. dog (video), Bruce Forsyth.
B) 1. open;2. pen; 3. far; 4. fun; 5. tug; 6. imp; 7. tear (perfume), Patsy Palmer. C) 1. tame; 2. dark; 3. pearl; 4. empty (tape), Bruce Samazan.
MISSING GOODIES:
Turkey.
SPOT SANTA:
A. Anneka Rice;
B. Shane Richie;
C. Penelope Keith.
CHRISSIE WORDS:
A. Tree; B. trifle;
C. reindeer;
D. snow;
E. holly.
SLEIGH BELLS:
Leaper.
OH, NO IT'S NOT!:
Aladdin;
Jack and the Beanstalk;
Cinderella;
Babes in the Wood;
Mother Goose.
CRIMBLY DECCIES:
H and C are the same.
FESTIVE NAME:
1. Salad; 2. apple; 3. night; 4. table; 5. adder.
CHRISSIE CROSSOUT:
Trifle.
CRACKING CRIMBO:
1. Santa; 2. carol; 3. cracker; 4. holly; 5. robin; 6. lights; 7. Rudolph; 8. sleigh; 9. present; 10. mistletoe; 11. bells; 12. candle; 13. star; 14. turkey; 15. tree; 16. card; 17. reindeer.
CHRISTMAS GUESTS:
A. Ronan (chocolates);
B. Jaason Simmons (books).

Well Made Up!

When best pals Lauren
ınd Nikela turned up at
ur make- over studio,
hey looked like two peas
n a pod! Even though they
ıadn't planned it, both
irls were wearing almost
xactly the same gear! So
ve chose lots of outfits
hat were the same but
lifferent!

AIR 'N' MAKE-UP

Lauren wanted curly hair, so ıake-up artist, Suzanne, used eated rollers. Lauren wouldn't ave her photo taken with them!

While the rollers were doing ıeir stuff, Suzanne did Nikela's ıake-up. Nikela has lovely skin, o all that was needed was a light usting of powder and blusher, natural brown shadow to elp emphasise the eyes and a lick of pale pink lip gloss. Two oats of mascara made Nikela's yes look wide and bright.

Lauren's make-up was almost he same. Suzanne explained hat the face powder stops you ooking shiny in the photos, and he eyeshadow and blusher stops he strong lights from draining ll the colour from your face. All ery technical!

When the rollers cooled, uzanne took them out and osened Lauren's curls ith her fingers. ikela had ovely, shiny air, so it was rushed through, nd Suzanne ecided just to se hairclips and crunchies to change he style.

The first outfit was cool for school or a summer day out. They were all from the same range, so pals can choose matching gear that isn't exactly the same.

Suzanne put hairclips in Lauren's hair and plaited Nikela's hair, finishing off with a gingham scrunchie.

Lauren thought the clogs were dead cool and Nikela liked her daisy print shoes, too.

LAUREN
White T-shirt — **£7,** navy skirt — **£8,** navy sweat top — **£16** and crochet bag — **£8,** all from Bhs. Clogs — **£12.99,** Dolcis. Hairclips — **£1.50** a pair, Tammy at Etam.

NIKELA
Navy dress — **£15,** Bhs. Daisy print shoes — **£8** and checked bag — **£7,** both Tammy at Etam. Scrunchies — **£3.50** (for 3), Marks and Spencer.

These outfits are great for shopping or hanging out with your mates. Lauren and Nikela liked these ones a lot and they both looked great in the pinky red shades.

NIKELA

Stripy long sleeved T-shirt — £13 and checked jeans — £15, both from Marks and Spencer. Red denim waistcoat — £12, Bhs. Heart print shoes — £8, Tammy at Etam.

LAUREN

Little Miss Splendid T-shirt — £8, Marks and Spencer. Red stretch trousers — £13, Bhs. White canvas shoes — £7.99, Dolcis.

Lauren and Nikela loc brill in these brightly coloure out 'n' about clothes. We made them work hard for these photos by getting them to blow big bubbles!

NIKELA

Red polo top — **£7,** Marks and Spence Leggings — **£6,** Tammy at Etam. Jacke with yellow lining — **£25** and flower hairclips — **£2** a pair, Bhs. Shoes — **£39.99,** Dolcis.

LAUREN

Yellow polo top — **£7** and scrunchies **£3.50** (for 3), both from Marks and Spencer. Jacket with navy lining — **£2** and navy stretch trousers — **£13,** both Bhs. Suede trainers — **£24.99,** Dolcis.

LAUREN
Lime silky touch mac — £25, orange flowery leggings — £9 and satin scrunchies — £2 (for 3) all Bhs. Lime cotton jumper — £15, Marks and Spencer. Sling-back shoes — £27.99, Dolcis.

NIKELA
Pink shiny mac — £30, pink striped top — £7, pink leggings — £7 and checked hat — £6, all from Bhs. Shoes — £17.99, Dolcis.

Some bright 'n' funky gear that's great for a disco or brightening up a dull day.

Best Bits About The Day

Lauren

My curly hair and funky bunches.
Blowing bubbles!
Trying on all those clothes.
Laughing at Nikela's pink shiny coat!

Nikela

Having my make-up done.
All the shoes were great.
Having a laugh with Lauren.

Worst Bits

Lauren

Going home!

Nikela

The pink shiny mac. I'd never dare wear that outside!

Coincidences

ONE day, when Ruth was out shopping —

Mmmm, he's nice! Pity he's going the other way!

In fact he was *REALLY* nice. Maybe I should go back up myself and try to see him again . . .

Nah, that would be daft. I mean, following someone you don't even know!

Then, next day —
There's that guy again — but he's *STILL* going the opposite way!

And now he's gone! I'm sure he smiled at me as he passed, though. Oh, I've just *GOT* to see him again!

Ruth told her mate, Bev.
. . . so I haven't a clue where he lives or anything. But he was in the mall yesterday. I'm gonna look there again tomorrow. Maybe he goes there every day.

Next day —
Did you go to the mall? Was he there?
Yes, I went. But there was no sign of him anywhere.

But later —
That's him — there!
BOOK

And that weekend —
There he is again! My *PLANS* to see him didn't work out, but I still keep seeing him just by coincidence!
Maybe it's fate. Sounds more romantic.

A few days later —
You look miserable. I assume you haven't seen him today then?
I have, actually. But it's always just passing and I'm getting sick of it.

I mean, what's the point of spotting him for a few seconds if I'm never going to get talking to him? Nothing ever happens. Maybe I should just forget it.

Hmm. Probably you *SHOULD* forget him. I'm going to a party later — come with me.

It's Simon's — you know, my brother's mate. You used to like him before you saw this other boy.
Yeah, but . . .

But *NOTHING!* If you don't come, you'll just sit at home moping about *HIM* and what good will that do?
Okay, you win. You're so *BOSSY!*

Later —
I'm not in a party mood. I know I should forget him, but I'm not sure I can. I still have this feeling he's special.
Wait till you see Simon again!
And —
Hi, Ruth! I'm glad you're here!
Hi, Simon!
Bev was right, I used to like Simon a lot . . .

. . . but not now. Not
after whatshisname.

It's mad. I can't get that other boy out of my
mind, but I don't even know his name! I think
I'll go home . . .

But —
Hey, don't walk out
on me *AGAIN!*
Oh — it's *YOU!* The
mystery boy!

Yeah, my name's David.
I'm Simon's cousin.

And —
. . . so I had to be bullied into coming here. I
didn't feel like it. I was fed up cos I kept seeing
you — but you always disappeared! At least
we've met now. And you say you almost didn't
come tonight either? What a *COINCIDENCE!*

Yeah, coincidences
are *GREAT!*
THE END.

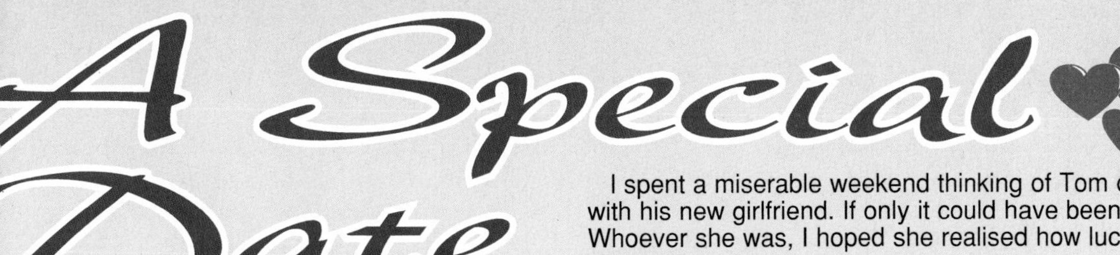

A Special Date

'D fancied Tom for ages, but he never seemed to notice me. Then, one night at the youth club, he came over to speak to me and I was thrilled.

Can I ask you something, Carrie?" he began.

My stomach turned a sort of somersault. He was ng to ask me out! After weeks of fancying him, he s finally going to ask me out!

Sure! Go ahead!" I replied, trying to sound cool.

Well, the thing is . . ." Tom hesitated, as if he n't know quite what to say. Then suddenly his rds came out in a rush.

There's this girl I want to take out," he explained. he's really special, so I don't want to make a mess hings, but I don't know what to do — where to e her and stuff. I was wondering if you'd give me ne advice."

felt sick inside. I'd got my hopes up for nothing. m didn't want to ask *me* out at all. And en worse, he wanted my help to get neone else! I couldn't bear it! I nted to tell him to get lost, but he ked at me so pleadingly and I ve in.

Okay. I'll help you," I heard self saying. "What do you nt to know?"

Where should I take her?" m asked eagerly.

sighed, trying to imagine self out on a first date with m — not that it was ever ng to happen now. Where uld I want to go? The disco or ema would be nice, but there uldn't be much chance to chat, d — on a first date with Tom — new I'd want to talk so I could to know him better.

How about going for a pizza?" uggested.

Great idea! Now, would a ek day or weekend be tter?"

Weekend," I replied. "Too ch homework during the ek!"

Right," Tom replied happily. ne other thing — what about thes? Smart or casual?"

He looked so gorgeous in jeans and denim shirt that ad no hesitation in ciding. "Casual," I said nly.

I spent a miserable weekend thinking of Tom out with his new girlfriend. If only it could have been me. Whoever she was, I hoped she realised how lucky she was.

The next week at the youth club, I half expected him to turn up with her, but he didn't. I felt a tiny ray of hope. Maybe she'd turned him down! In which case, there might still be a chance for me. I had to know! I walked over to Tom.

"How did your date go?" I asked, trying hard to sound casual.

"I haven't been yet," he replied. "It's this weekend. It's all set."

My heart sank.

"In fact, I've done everything except ask the girl," Tom continued. "I thought I'd do that tonight."

So my rival was someone at youth club! I looked sadly round the room. It was probably Cheryl, I decided — she's dead pretty. Or maybe Emma, who's really lively, or even Karen . . .

I was so busy looking round at them all and wondering who was the lucky one, that I didn't hear the next thing Tom said at first. I had to ask him to repeat it.

"Will you come to the pizza place with me?"

I gawped. "*Me?* But I thought you had some special girl you wanted to ask!"

"I did. It was you all along," he explained. "That's why I asked you to decide everything.

"You will come, won't you?" he added anxiously.

My face broke into a grin. "Yes, I'll come!" I replied. "I'd love to!"

And, as he grinned back at me, I knew it was going to be a really special date!

The Stars

ARIES
(March 22-April 20)

LIFE: When someone gets on the wrong side of you, you won't find it easy to forgive and forget. Don't worry, though — you'll eventually come to terms with things. In April you'll make a new friend who will be around for a long time.
SCHOOL: You'll breeze through exams this year because you'll be determined to do extra homework. You'll still be in trouble with teachers for talking too much, so be warned.
LURVE: The only guy you'll go out with will be clever, good looking, great fun and good company, too! Wow! In September, a girl will try to make you jealous, but it won't work.
LUCKY MONTH: JANUARY

TAURUS
(April 21-May 21)

LIFE: In the autumn, peeps you're close to will move far away and you'll realise how much they meant to you. You'll soon be smiling again when a fave Old of yours makes a surprising announcement.
SCHOOL: A new teacher could make school seem much more interesting to you. You'll take time with your work and do a great job with any project you undertake. Watch out for small probs in spring.
LURVE: Chances are you'll fall for a guy who's not the type you usually go for. He'll be really different from you. Opposites attract, you know!
LUCKY MONTH: NOVEMBER

GEMINI
(May 22-June 21)

LIFE: You've lots of friends and you'll have even more in the months ahead. You're kind and helpful and people like you. There are going to be big changes in your life in spring.
SCHOOL: You know that you do a lot of dreaming in class and this could cause probs for you. Homework will be piling up, so get on with it and don't moan about it.
LURVE: You'll hear rumours that a guy likes you — but don't believe everything your mates tell you. They like winding you up.
LUCKY MONTH: FEBRUARY

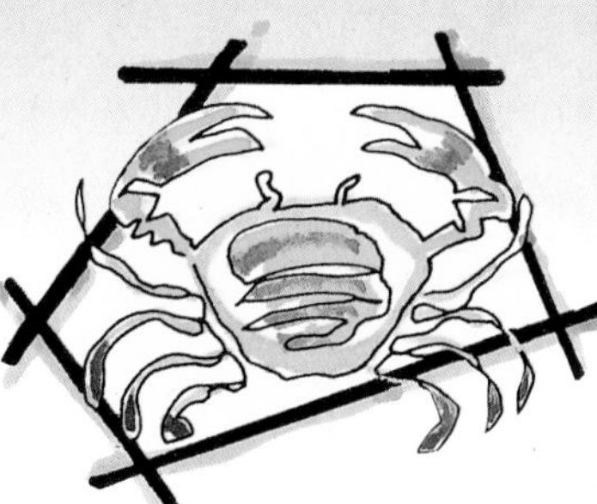

CANCER
(June 22-July 2

LIFE: Chances are you'll decide on a change of image in summer with interes results. You'll find th whole year a big adventure and you'll learn loads of new things.
SCHOOL: You'll get really involved in school activities and clubs. Through them you'll make new friends and might even come t work harder at your not-so-good subjects.
LURVE: A new romance could be coming. You may be able to believe how much you have in common wi certain guy.
LUCKY MONTH: OCTOBER

LEO
(July 24-Aug. 23)

LIFE: This year you'll have to make quite a few hard decisions, but you'll be given plenty of advice — just don't listen to it all! There's a possibility you'll be pressured into taking sides in a big row.
SCHOOL: You'll do some thinking about your future and you'll impress yo Olds with some test results.School will be a happy pl for you.
LURVE: A certain guy, who can make your day just b smiling at you, will become a good friend. Make the m of it!
LUCKY MONTH: JUNE

VIRGO
(Aug. 24-Sept. 2

LIFE: Plan ahead an there could be your b ever summer waiting you. A family membe will need your help badly towards the en of the year.
SCHOOL: Doing wh you're told immediat has never been your strong point, but try hard this year. It will be very muc for your own good to improve your grades.
LURVE: You might get annoyed when a boy wants to spend too much time with you when you want to see your mates.
LUCKY MONTH: APRIL

oretell

What's in store for you in the months ahead? Read on to find out!

IBRA
ept. 24-Oct. 23)

FE: A few family probs
uld upset you in spring
d you'll be glad of a
end's advice. Once
ngs are sorted out,
u'll be the centre of
tention and have a
eat social life.
HOOL: You may
ve a few sleepless
ghts because of some trouble in the classroom.
owever, confide in a teacher and everything will be
ickly sorted out.
JRVE: A few guys might catch your eye, but there
n't be anybody special. Relax, have a laugh and you'll
joy yourself.
JCKY MONTH: SEPTEMBER

SCORPIO
(Oct. 24-Nov. 22)

LIFE: There are going to be some big changes in your life — and all for the better. In winter, be on the look-out for a friend who needs help.
SCHOOL: You'll realise your schoolmates are keeping a secret from you and you'll feel left
t. Don't worry — eventually you'll understand what it's
about.
JRVE: You might suspect a guy of not being honest
th you. Unless you can prove it, you might be better off
eping quiet.
JCKY MONTH: JULY

AGITTARIUS
lov. 23-Dec. 22)

FE: Towards the middle
the year, you might
gin to grow away from
me of your friends when
u develop new interests.
n't worry — you'll make
w friends who'll like the
me things as you.
HOOL: Chances are a
acher will be very
pressed with some of your ideas. Believe it or not,
u'll probably begin to really enjoy school.
JRVE: You could make it difficult for a guy by being
ody. He could give you up because of it, so be
rned.
JCKY MONTH: MAY

CAPRICORN
(Dec. 23-Jan. 22)

LIFE: You do more travelling than usual this year — and you'll lurve every moment of it. Watch out for a mate's jealousy, though! She may try to spoil things for you during the summer holidays. Be prepared.
SCHOOL: A new girl in the class might need your help to settle in. Give it willingly and she could become a good friend.
LURVE: Your lurve life will be a bit quiet until a lad with a great sense of humour impresses you so much that you'll want to get to know him better.
LUCKY MONTH: DECEMBER

AQUARIUS
(Jan. 23-Feb. 19)

LIFE: Your year will get off to quite a slow start and you could feel a little low for a while. When March arrives, it will be all change. You might even be a lot richer! In the summer, you will have to come to the defence of a good mate.
SCHOOL: Your very good memory will serve you well, but a disagreement with a nasty classmate could upset you for a while.
LURVE: Someone will try to cause trouble between you and the guy you like. Don't get angry — just ignore it and it will blow over within days.
LUCKY MONTH: MARCH

PISCES
(Feb. 20-March 21)

LIFE: There's a very happy time ahead for you. You'll have loadsa friends and you'll be looking really great. August's the month for entering competitions and you should do well in at least one of them.
SCHOOL: You'll try harder at subjects you're not so good at with excellent results. Don't overdo things though. Try to balance work with fun and you'll really enjoy school.
LURVE: A guy will show an interest in you, but you won't be sure how you feel about him. Don't rush into anything.
LUCKY MONTH: AUGUST

Sam Kratz
RICHARD GRIEVE

Hannah Martin
REBECCA RITTERS

NEIGHBOURS

SEPTEMBER

MONDAY	1	8	15	22	29
TUESDAY	2	9	16	23	30
WEDNESDAY	3	10	17	24	–
THURSDAY	4	11	18	25	–
FRIDAY	5	12	19	26	–
SATURDAY	6	13	20	27	–
SUNDAY	7	14	21	28	–

OCTOBER

MONDAY	–	6	13	20	27
TUESDAY	–	7	14	21	28
WEDNESDAY	1	8	15	22	29
THURSDAY	2	9	16	23	30
FRIDAY	3	10	17	24	31
SATURDAY	4	11	18	25	–
SUNDAY	5	12	19	26	–

NOVEMBER

MONDAY	–	3	10	17	24
TUESDAY	–	4	11	18	25
WEDNESDAY	–	5	12	19	26
THURSDAY	–	6	13	20	27
FRIDAY	–	7	14	21	28
SATURDAY	1	8	15	22	29
SUNDAY	2	9	16	23	30

DECEMBER

MONDAY	1	8	15	22	29
TUESDAY	2	9	16	23	30
WEDNESDAY	3	10	17	24	31
THURSDAY	4	11	18	25	–
FRIDAY	5	12	19	26	–
SATURDAY	6	13	20	27	–
SUNDAY	7	14	21	28	–

Danielle Stark ELIZA SZONERT

Mandy
FOR GIRLS
1997
STORIES
PUZZLE
PIN-U